SILVER BELLE

BOOK THREE OF THE GREEN SKY SERIES

JENNAE VALE

CHAPTER 1

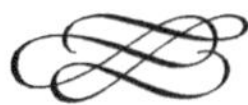

*S*he jingled as she walked. Silver coins adorning her ears, her wrists and hanging loosely around her waist and neck danced to a lilting rhythm announcing her approach with each step she took. Belle Silver, or Silver Belle as she was known by her ship's crew, was a pirate both feared and admired by those who knew her. Any man who doubted her reputation and dared challenge her found themselves at the tip of her sword begging forgiveness and offering her whatever silver they might possess to avoid her wrath. Her ship, *The Enchantress,* was safely moored in the harbor. Most of her crew had joined her in port, leaving a small number of men behind to be relieved later.

Belle had a lot on her mind. She was being pursued by an English naval vessel and had been lucky enough to lose them during a storm the night before. It was the closest they'd ever come to *The Enchantress* and Belle knew it was only a matter of time before she was caught and brought back to England to be tried for crimes against the crown.

In her forty years on earth, Belle had always loved a good adventure, but the English had been breathing down her neck these past months, turning those adventures into a run for her life and putting the lives of her crew members in great danger. She'd heard a wild story through the grapevine that Jameson Mackall had a connection with a witch who could help her evade capture and perhaps help her find the treasure that had once belonged to her father, John Silver. The map that would lead her to its hiding place was securely in her possession, just as her father intended. She had always planned on locating it when her pirating days were done. The treasure would afford her a life of luxury in her retirement, if she could find it before being caught.

Mackall's home here in St. George's was her destination. Belle hoped he'd be willing to help her and to that end she'd made some inquiries and gotten an address where he could be found.

The house she sought was in sight. The two-story pink manor with a white roof had a small balcony on the second floor that over-looked the front door. Towering palm trees stood guard on either side of the cobbled pathway leading to the entrance. Eight multi-paned windows gave the occupants a good view of approaching visitors and Belle suspected someone inside had seen or heard her approach. The suspicion was confirmed when the door opened before she could even lift the knocker.

"Good day to you, Madame." The footman who opened the door didn't seem the least surprised to see her, despite her silver laden garb.

"I'd like to see Jameson Mackall," she tipped her head and an uncharacteristic almost-a-smile appeared on her lips. She wasn't sure it would work but it was her best effort to not look like the fearsome pirate she was.

"Right this way." The man led her through the house to a door at the back which opened onto a beautiful garden.

Belle took a moment to admire the flowers and fruit trees that seemed to be everywhere. There were so many that it was hard to believe there might be room for anything else. The footman led her down another cobbled path like the one in the front of the house, curving through the trees and plants before ending in a small open area. There she spied Jameson Mackall sitting with two women, each holding beverages and seeming surprised to see her.

Jameson stood first. "Belle Silver! To what do we owe the honor of yer presence?"

Nervously, she shifted her weight from one foot to the other. On the tip of her tongue were words she hated saying. In all her years as a pirate she hadn't uttered them once. The fact that she had to do so now galled her to no end. "I need your help."

If Jameson was surprised by her admission, he hid it well. "Harold, bring our guest a drink please." Jameson turned to the women. "This is Belle Silver, daughter of the legendary John Silver. Belle is rather legendary in her own right. Belle, this is me wife Danielle and this is Lady Charlotte, the owner of this beautiful manor."

"It's so nice to meet you," Danielle said. Her eyes showed she was curious, but her smile was warm and genuine.

Lady Charlotte echoed Danielle's greeting, though a bit more reserved.

"Danielle, why don't we go inside and leave these two to talk," Lady Charlotte suggested.

"Of course." Danielle stood and the two walked the cobbled path back to the house. Their voices carrying on the breeze as they went.

"What do you suppose she wants?" Danielle asked.

"I don't know, my dear," Lady Charlotte answered, peeking back over her shoulder.

"She'd better not ask him to go on any voyages with her," Danielle said.

Belle sat in the chair that Jameson indicated and regarded him from across the table.

Jameson met her gaze with a warm smile, "I've retired from pirating."

"I've heard," Belle said, feeling uncomfortable and fidgeting with the edge of her coat.

As far as pirates were concerned, Jameson Mackall was more trustworthy than most. He was a handsome man and one her father had warned her away from. John Silver wanted his daughter to marry someone of stature in London but try as he might, she resisted. He never wanted her to follow in his footsteps, but Belle wasn't one to allow anyone, even the great John Silver, to tell her how she should live her life.

Belle was very good at taking care of herself and her crew, but for once in her life she felt vulnerable, and it stung. Asking for help from anyone at all was not something that came naturally. But over the years, she'd crossed paths with Jameson—they had even plundered a ship or two in partnership with each other. He had always been a man of his word and now it seemed he had also become an honest man. It was the only reason she felt she could consider sharing her story with him.

"Where to begin? Hmmm…" The words stuck in her throat. It was best to just say what she'd come to say so she squared her shoulders and looked him dead in the eye. "I'm in trouble. A British warship has been bearing down on me. There's an officer aboard that has sworn a vendetta against me and so for the safety of my ship and crew, it is best that I disappear for a while but I've nowhere safe to go."

"'Tis why I've retired," Jameson said. His lips curled in a sympathetic smile.

"I've one last treasure to find, and then I can retire somewhere they'll never find me."

"Aye. There's always one last treasure," Jameson said, with a knowing smile.

Belle huffed a laugh at the truth. "This one is my father's. After he died, a map was given to me by his first mate. He told me that my father wanted me to have it, and so it is mine and mine alone. My inheritance, if you will. I must find it. When I do, I will be satisfied." She was quite sure she would be, even though Jameson was looking at her with some skepticism.

"Ye said ye needed me help. I'm no' sure what ye might need from me, but as long as it doesnae entail boarding a ship to help ye search, I'd be happy to do what I can." Jameson picked up his drink and leaned back in his chair. He took a sip as he waited for her to speak.

Belle took in a deep breath and then blew it out along with the words she'd been repeating over and over again in her head. There was an excellent chance Jameson would think her a daft fool for even thinking the rumors were true and she would never live it down. "I've been told there's a witch who might be able to help me and that you know where to find her."

"Ye mean Morwenna," Jameson said. "Aye. I ken where she is most o' the time."

Belle was relieved to hear that there really was a witch. "Is she nearby?"

"She has a small cottage on the beach but she's no' always there. She travels to Charleston often."

"Charleston, you say." She tapped her chin with her forefinger as she thought. If she had to make a run for Charleston she could, though the chances of her making it were slim.

"What exactly have ye heard about Morwenna?" he asked.

"She can make you disappear from the island and appear in another place."

Jameson nodded, "And another time."

It's what she'd heard, but she hadn't wanted to say it out loud. "Aye. Another time."

Jameson studied at her for a moment, seeming to examine Belle before addressing her in a thoughtful manner. "Do ye wish to travel to a different time? To the future perhaps?" he asked.

Belle had been thinking about this ever since she'd heard about the witch. She thought that if it would help in her quest to escape capture, she would consider it. Afterall, she had always been able to blend in seamlessly when in different ports. It was a skill she'd learned from her father and one a pirate would be wise to master. She'd even donned the occasional disguise when it had been of use to her. If she were to travel through time, she had no doubt she would do well wherever she ended up. "I must get off this island. I believe it is the only way to save myself. I'll turn *The Enchantress* over to the crew. They'll pick a new captain and rename the ship. And I shall disappear."

"They doona wish to disappear as well?" Jameson asked.

"Nay. That navy scallywag is only interested in me. They will be fine without me." The men of *The Enchantress* were a wily bunch, but their chances of avoiding conflict with the warship that was after Belle were better if they were on their own. They understood this and while leaving her ship and crew had been the hardest decision of her life, it was one she made for the benefit of all involved. She would miss her life aboard *The Enchantress*, but this was for the best.

"I'm surprised ye'd give up so easily." Jameson leaned forward, resting his forearms on his knees and gazing at her with what seemed genuine curiosity.

Belle gazed off into the distance. The birds in a far-off tree were singing happily but were hidden among the leaves making it impossible to see them. She wished to be like them. Happy and safely hidden. "I've been pirating a long time. Too long perhaps. I've been lucky, but I feel my luck is running out."

"'Tis how I felt when I decided to retire."

"Are you safe here?" Belle wondered.

Jameson sat back once again and glanced around at the garden and then the house. "I am, but I know that if I ever need to leave, Morwenna will help me. She helped Edward Sutherland not so long ago, he's in Charleston now."

"Sutherland? I wondered where he's been. I haven't seen him in a very long time." Edward Sutherland had been Jameson's quartermaster for many years. She'd heard that he disappeared, but no one seemed to know what had happened to him. Now she knew. Morwenna had helped him.

Belle drew in a deep breath. She wasn't sure Charleston was the place for her. Yes, there were pirates there, but there was also a strong British military presence. She wasn't sure that would work for her.

"I can tell ye ken the reputation of the city. I should mention, Edward lives in the year 2022. The British are no longer a concern there."

A city free from the British? That was a dream come true. "Where do I find Morwenna?"

"I'll take ye to her. Would ye like to go now?"

"I would." If she was going to do this, it was best done quickly. If she stayed any longer, she feared she might put Jameson and his entire household in danger.

Jameson called to Harold. "Get the carriage ready."

"What if she's not there?" Belle asked, feeling uncharacteristically nervous.

"I choose to hope she is. If she's no', ye can stay here until she returns. I'll speak with Lady Charlotte."

"She's a friend to the pirates, or so I've heard."

"I believe if she could, she'd be one herself." Jameson chuckled as he stood and beckoned for Belle to follow him.

On the street outside of the manor stood a black carriage adorned with gold ornamentation on the doors and around the windows.

Harold stood waiting for them. He opened the carriage door and Belle entered, followed by Jameson. "We'd like to go to Morwenna's cottage, Harold."

"Sir." Harold bowed his head as he closed the carriage door before climbing atop the coach.

A warm breeze floated through the open carriage window reminding Belle what it was that she loved about the Caribbean. England would be cold and damp at this time of year, but as with most of the places she sailed, the climate here was tropical year-round.

Gazing out the window at the passing palm trees, she wondered about her fate. Traveling to the future hadn't been her plan. She merely wished to locate her father's treasure, but it seemed that fate had other plans for her if she wished to remain a free woman.

"Are ye worried?" Jameson asked.

The last thing she wanted was for anyone to think she was worried or afraid. She was Belle Silver, fearless pirate who'd come face-to-face with danger more often than most. "Of course not."

"Good. I've time traveled, ye ken. I've visited Edward in Charleston. The future, while no' for me, may suit ye, Belle."

She hadn't given time travel much thought until this moment. Her mind was fully on the treasure and outsmarting the English warship that had been following her. But if there was any way that she could vanish from this time for a period of months, or even years until the English forgot about her, then that would suit her just fine. Although sooner rather than later would be her preference. It was good to know that Jameson had been able to return from his trip to the future. It meant she would be able to as well.

The carriage bumped along the heavily rutted road until it stopped without warning. Belle glanced out the window to see the ocean waves crashing upon the shore. The tide was coming in and a breeze off the water offered the scent of salty air and the sea.

"Are ye sure ye wish to do this?" Jameson asked.

"Aye." She opened the carriage door and hopped out onto the sand, her boots sinking in as she landed.

Jameson stayed where he was. "That's her cottage there. I'll wait for ye here. If she's no' home come back, and we'll try again on another day. If she's there, I wish ye well."

"Thank you." Belle chose to ignore the tightness in her chest as she trod past the horses to the door of the small cottage. She knocked and waited a short moment before she heard a woman's voice.

"Come in, if you please," the woman said.

Belle turned and waved to the carriage driver, letting him know they could return home. Opening the door, she found the woman, Morwenna, lounging on a quilted hammock by the window.

"Are you Morwenna?" Belle asked.

"Who wishes to know?" The woman stayed where she was.

"Belle Silver. I've been told you can help me."

"I'm Morwenna." As she swung her legs out of the hammock so that she sat facing Belle, her eyebrows lifted in recognition of the name. "And what could Silver Belle possibly need from me?"

"I want to go where Edward Sutherland is." She had given it some thought and decided that if she was going to leave this time it would be good to know at least one person where she'd be headed. "And I need some help finding my father's treasure. It is of the utmost importance."

"Why Sutherland? Do you love him or wish to kill him?" Morwenna eyed her with some suspicion.

Belle couldn't help but laugh. What an absurd thought. The only one who could love Edward Sutherland was the man himself. His ego allowed no room for anyone else. "Neither. He is an old acquaintance. I must escape the British before I am arrested for piracy. As I said, finding the treasure is my priority."

Morwenna laughed, seemingly reading Belle's mind and ignoring what she'd said about the treasure not once but twice. "Seems a good enough reason as any. It's a good thing you're not in love. Edward's married, you know. I don't wish to help you ruin that and it's good you don't wish to kill him. I could not condone such actions."

"Married?" Belle stifled another laugh. She couldn't believe her ears and couldn't imagine who would have Edward, for that matter.

Morwenna nodded her head as she chuckled. It seemed she found the thought of Edward being married as amusing as Belle did. She was strange, but why wouldn't she be? She was a witch. Belle had never had occasion to meet a witch before this, or at least she wasn't aware that she had.

"You are in luck, Miss Silver. I have been planning a trip to that exact time. You may accompany me."

"I believe my treasure is buried on the mainland. That is where we're going, isn't it?" Belle asked.

"Treasure, treasure. That's all you pirates seem to think about. Worry not. I'll take you where you wish to go and perhaps you can enlist the help of Mr. Sutherland in your quest to find this treasure." Morwenna scanned the room before turning her attention back to Belle.

Belle thought about her treasure map and Edward Sutherland in the same room. She would absolutely not be asking for his help. A momentary sense of unease hit Belle as she noted Morwenna staring at her. She had no idea what was about to happen or where she'd end up. Belle was used to being the one to set the course, but in this instance she was giving up control to Morwenna. It wasn't easy letting go as the thought of journeying through time suddenly became very real.

"There's no need for you to fear a thing," Morwenna said.

"I fear nothing," Belle growled.

Morwenna snickered. "Exactly as I thought." The witch gathered items around the room and deposited them in a cloth bag set atop a table. Once everything had been collected, she said something Belle couldn't quite hear and then reached into a cabinet to extract a rock. "Here, you hold this."

Belle took the rock from her, examining it. Sand and sea merged in a swirl on the stone that fit neatly in the palm of her hand.

"Take my hand if you don't mind." Morwenna held out her hand.

Belle switched the stone into her other hand and reached for Morwenna with her now free hand. The witch grasped it with a grip so tight it almost took Belle's breath away.

"So sorry. I don't wish to lose you on the way. I've just the one rock you see. This is the magic we need to travel, so don't drop it." She adjusted the cloth bag over her shoulder and began chanting in a language that was foreign to Belle, who was now grasping the rock with the same strength Morwenna was using to hold her hand.

The ground beneath them quaked and rolled as all went dark around them. Belle wished to speak, but her voice would not come out. Where were they? What was happening? None of the words left her lips and then before she could try again, it all stopped, and they were still in the same cottage they'd been in moments before.

"What happened? We're still here," Belle said.

"I take my home with me when I travel, but I leave a replica behind for those who seek to find me. They know if I'm not home that I'm away and will return."

"So, we're there? Where the treasure is hidden?" She placed her hand in her pocket and fingered the map she'd kept there since her father's death.

"Of course we're here," Morwenna said. "Did you doubt me? As for the treasure, you'll have to find that yourself." She opened her bag.

"Drop the stone inside. I've given far too many of these away. I'll tend this one and if you need to return to your time, seek me out here."

Belle did as she was instructed and watched as Morwenna replaced everything she'd set in the bag back around the cottage. Not sure what to do next, she stood there feeling very much the same as she had a short while ago. "Thank you."

"You're welcome. You may go. If I don't see you again, make yourself a good life here."

CHAPTER 2

*B*elle walked out the door of Morwenna's cottage and onto the sandy path that led away from it. Glancing around her, things seemed very much the same. A small cottage on the beach. The waves crashing against the shore. She began to walk. Unsure of where exactly she was headed, she allowed her inner sailor to chart her course. She continued her path along the shoreline, passing houses that were quite grand but not seeing a single soul as she walked.

It was now close to sunset on this early December day. Letting her instincts guide her Belle's first thought was to find shelter. If she couldn't find an inn, then she would sleep on the beach. It wouldn't be the first time she'd made camp on the sand. It occurred to her that she had no idea what year it was, but did it really matter? Wherever she'd landed was to be her home for the time being and under the circumstances, she would settle in as comfortably as she could. Having brought a bag of silver with her would allow her to secure accommodations until such time as she knew just how a pirate would manage to live in this time. She might have to hunt down Edward Sutherland for advice on such matters. That is, if she had landed in the Charleston of the time he resided in.

As the sun finally set, Belle wrapped her arms around herself to ward off the now chilly air and left the sandy beach behind. She could see lights not too far off in the distance. There was something different about them and as she got closer she could see that they were brighter than any she'd seen in her time and there were so many of them. Not a torch was to be seen anywhere. The buildings looked the same for the most part, although there were some that were quite unusual. The sand path she'd been on had become a much harder, solid surface. She'd examine it further in the morning when the sun had risen. Her focus now was to find a place to stay for the night and a meal to appease the grumbling of her belly.

Masts of ships appeared and Belle headed toward them. But as she approached she realized none of them looked like the ships she'd left behind in Bermuda. Instead of brown wood, their masts stood tall and bright white in contrast to the dark blue of the sky. She marveled at the shiny hulls of the other mastless boats that also filled the harbor. There were so many of them it was hard to believe.

So many questions plagued her mind, but most were about her treasure. She was sure it was on the mainland and in or near Charleston, as her father had been in that area many times. She reached into her pocket and took out the map. Examining it now, she wasn't quite so sure. Nothing on it looked like the Charleston she knew. Her father was a clever man and he would have drawn a map that would throw anyone finding it off the track. Only he knew where this treasure was buried and he was no longer around to help Belle find it. Being John Silver's daughter had its advantages, though, the most important of which was understanding the way he thought. Even without her father, Belle was confident she would find it. It was what he wanted for her. She carefully placed the map back in her pocket and continued on her way into an area that was bustling with activity.

Glancing around her at shops filled with things she'd never seen before, Belle stopped for a moment to take it all in. Each shop had a sign with its name, and all were lit from within with more of the bright lights she'd seen on the street. The windows were decorated with more colorful lights and things that reminded her it was going to be Christmas soon. The streets were filled with people dressed in strange clothing. Some stared at her as she passed, pointing at her and conversing with their companions. Carriages without horses made strange sounds as they sped past. The atmosphere was quite festive as the people, young and old, seemed to be genuinely enjoying themselves.

A small lad stopped in front of her, his fingers sticky from candy he held tightly in his grip. Staring up at her, he quickly glanced around for his mother. She nodded to him. "It's okay to ask," she said.

"Are you a pirate?" he asked.

Belle couldn't help it. A smile briefly lit her lips before she answered. "I am. How did you know?"

He shrugged his little shoulders. "You look like one."

Belle bowed slightly in his direction and he did the same back to her.

His mother laughed. "Thank you. He loves pirates."

"We are not a loveable lot," Belle responded.

The little boy wandered away and his mother followed. "I love how she stayed in character," she said to a woman who walked with her.

"Character! Pfft!" Belle shook her head in disgust at the thought that she played some role.

Continuing on her way towards the marina and the boats, Belle rounded a corner and was stopped in her tracks as she spied an unbelievable sight. It was *The Dagger*. Hadn't she just seen it in Bermuda when she'd docked *The Enchantress*? Confusion mixed with apprehension as she wondered if she'd been tricked by the witch. Was she still in Bermuda? No. She was in Charleston. All of the sights she'd just seen told her that. The witch had brought her. It was *The Dagger* that was out of place

There had to be some explanation for *The Dagger's* appearance in this harbor at this time. She marched towards it determined to find the answer. When she reached the ship, Belle stood at the foot of the gangplank eyeing the path upward. Before ascending she glanced over her shoulder. Always on guard for anyone who might be following her or laying in wait, Belle felt more ill-at-ease in this new world than she ever had in all her travels aboard *The Enchantress*. Shrugging off the natural suspicion creeping up her spine, Belle strode up towards the main deck. Upon reaching it she spotted a woman dressed in the unfamiliar garb of this time.

It was obvious the woman heard her arrive because she turned, eyeing Belle with a wide smile and a wave, leaving Belle baffled as to how to respond. No one had ever greeted Belle Silver this way. The suspicion she'd tried to rid herself of returned as she placed her hand on the hilt of her cutlass.

The woman approached, seemingly unaware of Belle's wary posture and readiness to react quickly to any perceived threat.

"Hello," the woman said. "You're a little late for a tour of the ship. We open again tomorrow morning at ten."

Belle eyed her through narrowed slits, her stance shifting to one only slightly less threatening. The woman hardly seemed to notice as she approached and whether she knew it or not, she had placed herself in real danger.

"I love your costume," the woman said as she looked Belle over from head-to-toe.

Belle glanced down at herself, feeling somewhat insulted. "These are my clothes, not a costume." This was the second time someone had accused her of playing a role.

"Oh, I'm so sorry. Forgive me." The woman took a step back, perhaps sensing something wasn't right. "Can I help you with something?"

"I'm in search of Edward Sutherland."

"Oh." She took another step away from Belle.

This woman knew where he was. She could read it in her wide-eyed stare and shifting stance. "Have you seen him?" Belle was in no mood for delay tactics.

"I have. He's here somewhere, but as I said, we're closed for the day." She glanced around seeming ill at ease.

"I care not whether you are closed. I will see Edward Sutherland and I will see him now." Belle moved closer one step, then two and with each step the woman did the same, retreating.

"I told you, I don't know where he is." She angled herself slightly away from Belle as if she might run.

"Where is he?" Belle repeated the question. Her voice was low and menacing. She was losing patience.

"I can't imagine what you'd want with Edward." The woman's voice took on a slight tremble as she spoke. She glanced around behind her before cursing softly beneath her breath.

Belle only wished to frighten her into talking, but it appeared more would be needed to further intimidate the woman into answering. She brandished her cutlass as she closed the distance to the visibly shaken woman who had now backed herself up against the ship's rail. Grabbing her by the arm, Belle held the cutlass inches from her throat. "I've asked you a question and you still have not answered me."

"My name is Susanna Sutherland," she stammered. "I'm Edward's wife." Susanna nodded towards the cutlass. "If you're planning to kill him then I'm definitely not going to tell you anything."

So this was the woman who'd married Sutherland. She was not what Belle had expected and certainly not the type of woman Edward was normally seen with or deserved. Despite her trembling, Susanna Sutherland had proven to be brave in her efforts to protect her husband. It was something Belle admired. "I've no desire to kill him. I was told to find him when I arrived."

Susanna shook her arm free from Belle's grip, straightened her shoulders and held her head high. It was obvious she was feeling more in control of the situation. She gazed at Belle from the perspective of a woman who had shaken off her fear and now understood the woman she was facing meant her husband no harm. After a moment and a few deep breaths, she seemed to relax enough to call out. "Edward!" she shouted. "Edward!"

"What is it love?" Edward Sutherland's voice came from below deck.

"There's someone here to see you and she says she's not planning to kill you, but I'm not so sure how she feels about me."

The thudding sounds of heavy footsteps running up the stairs announced Edward's arrival. As he reached the deck, sword in hand, he stopped dead in his tracks. "Belle? Belle Silver?" He moved closer, peering at her as if he'd seen a ghost. "Is it really you? What are you doing here?"

"Same as you I imagine." She eyed him with what little patience she had left. Edward Sutherland was a man she tolerated only when it was necessary. It was good to see a familiar face in this very strange place, although she would never say that to him.

"Is she from your time Edward?" Susanna asked in a whisper.

"She is." Edward moved to place himself between Susanna and Belle, though he lowered his sword in the process. It seemed polite to lower hers as well. "How did you know I was here?" His narrowed eyes showed his suspicion.

"Mackall told me," Belle said, feeling every bit as unsure of him as he was of her.

"Then you know I'm a married man. This is my wife, Susanna." He nodded to his wife who still stood behind him, but was inching her way around him to be part of the conversation.

"So she said." Belle stared at him in disbelief. "Do you really think that is why I am here?"

Susanna was now standing so that she could see her husband's face and like Belle seemed to be waiting for his answer.

"Why else would you be here?" he asked.

Belle couldn't help herself as laughter bubbled up from inside of her. "I can see marriage hasn't changed you much. You've always thought very highly of yourself, but this time you are sadly mistaken. I am not here for you." Belle shook her head. He was the last man she'd be interested in romantically. Belle sent a sympathetic look Susanna's way. She couldn't imagine how this poor woman ended up with Edward Sutherland. Living with him and his ego must be quite taxing.

They stood staring and sizing each other up for a few moments longer. Susanna for her part seemed somewhat amused by the situation as she glanced from one to the other and back again.

"Are you going to tell me why you're here?" he asked. His impatience was showing.

"I needed to disappear for a while. The English were getting a bit too close for comfort." She wasn't sure she should share the information about John Silver's treasure with Edward, so she left that part out.

"I imagine you need my help and a place to stay." Her presence seemed to have irritated him based on his testy reply.

She did need his help, but she wasn't about to admit it. She was alone here in an unfamiliar time and he was the only connection she had to her life in the past. "I don't need your help, but I could use a place to stay. If you could recommend something…"

"For how long?" Susanna interrupted.

"I'm not sure. Perhaps a month or two. Just long enough for them to give up on finding me." She hoped it wouldn't be for much longer, but had no way of knowing.

Susanna and Edward exchanged looks with each other.

"Two months would be a challenge, I think," Susanna said, sounding less than happy about it.

"At least," Belle answered. She turned to Edward. "If I remember correctly Sutherland, you are in my debt." If she had to use that bit of information to her advantage, she would.

"What?" Susanna asked, gazing at her husband.

"She may or may not have saved my life once," Edward said, not sounding the least bit grateful or happy about it.

"There is no may or may not. I did and that's all there is to it." The man was incorrigible.

"Fine. You've a place to stay for the time being." Edward gave Susanna what appeared to be an apologetic look. "Dinner is ready and waiting for us."

Susanna turned her attention to Belle. "Have you eaten?"

"I'm quite famished." It had been a while since she'd eaten.

Susanna gazed at Edward before lightly punching his arm.

"You'll join us then," Edward said. "Right this way. And Belle, put the cutlass away. You won't need it here."

He led the way down the stairs where Belle immediately could see that she was interrupting a romantic dinner for two.

"I'll get another place setting," Susanna said, heading into a small room that on most ships would be considered the entry to the larder, but on this one it seemed to hold plates, glasses and silverware.

"We'll eat first and then discuss how we're going to get you to fit in around here." Edward waved his hand up and down, indicating her clothing. "You can't walk around town with every piece of silver you own jangling loudly with every step you take."

Susanna returned and set a place for Belle. Bench seats on either side of the table, which was fastened to the wall, were covered with cushions—a fancy upgrade from the ships she was used to.

Edward and Susanna sat across from her. The food placed in the center of the table smelled delicious. Her mouth watered as Edward placed a large piece of fish on her plate along with roasted potatoes. Edward held up a bowl of greenery. "Salad?" he asked.

It was a rare day that fresh vegetables were available aboard ship. Belle was happy to take advantage of what was being offered. Taking a bite of fish, she was amazed at the flavor of the herbs and spices that had been combined to create one of the best things she had ever eaten. "This is quite good," she said, through a mouthful of food.

"Thank you," Edward said.

"Did you cook this?" she asked, giving him a sideways glance.

"I did."

"Edward likes to cook. It's a real passion for him," Susanna said, casting a proud smile in his direction.

"If I'd only known," Belle said, savoring the roasted potatoes and winking at Edward.

Susanna turned to Edward, spared a glance at Belle, then focused her attention on her husband once again. "Is there something you're not telling me, Edward?"

Edward scowled in Belle's direction before stumbling over his words. "It's…it's nothing of importance and certainly not anything for you to worry about."

"He's right. 'Twas but a night and nothing more." Belle was driving the stake through his heart. She hid her smile behind her napkin.

Susanna nearly choked on her drink. She gently set it down and stared at her husband. "A night? Now I think I have to know what you're talking about."

Belle exchanged a not so apologetic look with Edward, enjoying the trouble she could see brewing. If looks could kill, she'd surely be dead.

"We were drunk. I'm quite sure nothing happened," Edward said. He placed his knife and fork down before lifting the napkin from his lap to swipe at his mouth. "Belle would agree with me." He gazed at Belle with steely eyes. "Wouldn't you?"

Belle knew she could make Edward squirm even more if she really wanted to. She'd done it enough times in the past to know just how enjoyable it was. Instead she decided to be merciful. "Edward is right. We were much too drunk for anything to have transpired. The next morning we were occupying the same bed. It created quite a stir among the crew." Susanna's eyes were hard to read. "We were fully clothed, of course."

Susanna turned her head towards her husband, then seemed to decide something with a curt nod of her head. "Well, it was before we knew each other, Edward. We both have a past. I just never thought I'd meet yours."

"At one time I thought him quite handsome, but once I got to know him I realized he was a rake and nothing more. The kind of man my father had warned me about."

Susanna appeared a bit out of sorts. Perhaps she was offended to know her husband was considered a rake. "You're a pirate, am I right?"

Belle nodded as she popped a piece of roasted potato into her mouth.

"Your father warned you away from rakes, but not away from piracy?"

"Susanna, her father was the great John Silver," Edward said.

"Oh, I've actually heard of him," Susanna said, seeming pleased with that knowledge.

"My father sent me off to receive an education. The last thing he wished was for me to follow in his footsteps."

"But you did," Susanna stated.

"Of course. He wasn't happy about it, but once I was in command of *The Enchantress* he accepted it and was happy to advise me when needed." She wiped her mouth with the cloth napkin she'd been provided.

"*The Enchantress.* What a great name for a ship captained by a woman." It seemed Susanna was warming up to her. At least the woman didn't seem the type to hold a grudge.

"I thought so, too."

"What's going on with your ship?" Edward asked.

Uneasiness crept over her. "I've given it over to my crew. I did not wish to end up hanging from the gallows, but they are safe. It is me the English want. The crew will be safer with me gone." The thought of spending two months away from her ship was daunting. She hadn't spent so much time ashore since she was a child growing up in England with her mother. She would surely miss her ship and her crew.

"You'll be safe here. Even in your unusual attire. People won't bat an eye," Edward said. "The history of piracy is alive and well here."

"Where are your crew?" Belle asked, glancing around for any sign of them.

"At home with their families I would imagine," Edward said.

"Home? Don't they live aboard ship?" This was astounding news.

"No. I'm done with pirating. Although the people who visit Charleston can't seem to get enough of it. We set sail a few times a week with those who would pay for the pleasure of being aboard a pirate ship."

"We also rent the ship out for weddings and parties. In fact, we'll be having a large Christmas party in a few weeks." Susanna turned to Edward. "Which reminds me, Edward, we really need to get some trees and do some decorating."

"We'll get started tomorrow. I promise," he said.

"What am I to do? When I saw *The Dagger* here in the harbor, I envisioned sailing out to sea and plundering any unsuspecting ship we ran across."

"Things don't work that way in this time. There are no pirates like you here," Susanna said.

"No treasure?" Belle couldn't believe her ears. What godforsaken place had she landed in?

"Not what you're used to, but you can make a good life for yourself here." Edward poured them all more wine.

"You can work for us," Susanna said with a sideways glance at Edward. "People will love you. You're a far cry from the locals who work for us and dress in pirate costumes. You're the real deal."

"The real deal." She repeated not bothering to ask what that meant. To say she was disappointed would be an understatement. But on the other hand, what had she expected? It was obvious that there was no place in this world for a pirate queen such as herself. No matter, she wouldn't be here that long anyway. She would find the treasure, go back to her time and find a place far from the prying eyes of the English navy.

"I'll do it," Belle said. While she preferred to captain her own vessel, under the circumstances being second in command would have to do.

"Tomorrow we'll take you shopping. You'll need some clothes and we'll show you around town." Susanna's voice was filled with an enthusiasm Belle was lacking.

"Christmas is coming. Charleston is quite festive at this time of year. There will be a parade of ships, which is why we must decorate." Edward look a long sip of his wine, then wiped his mouth with his napkin.

"It's a big hit with the locals and tourists too." Susanna appeared quite excited by what she was saying.

Tourists? Decorating? Parades? Belle wondered how she would survive this self-imposed exile. It seemed Edward was a mind reader as he said, "You should just take the time to relax and not worry about things in the past. Lots of things will be happening around here that will be fun. You'll enjoy it."

"You seem quite sure of it," Belle said, lifting her glass and taking a rather large swig of her wine.

"I am," he assured her.

"You know I'm not the type to sit still for long." If she was forced to, she just might lose her mind.

"And you won't need to. There are plenty of things you can do," Edward said.

"Such as?" Belle asked.

It was obvious Edward didn't have an answer at the ready. "You'll see," he said. "Tomorrow morning we'll start getting you acclimated."

"I need some fresh air," Belle said. She stood and headed for the stairs that would lead her to the deck.

"I'll show you to your room when you're ready," Susanna called after her.

Already at the top of the stairs, Belle didn't bother to answer.

CHAPTER 3

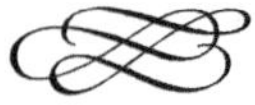

Belle walked to the rail of the ship's deck and gazed out over the harbor. Lights twinkled everywhere, dulling the stars of the night sky. One of the many things she enjoyed about being at sea was the deep black of the night sky with only the moon and stars to light the way. Small boats cruised through the waterway seemingly on their own power. This was truly an astonishing period. She would learn all she could before heading back to her own time. Sounds of music and people talking and laughing floated through the air. Belle wondered where the seamen of this time went once in port. Were there still taverns and inns where those like her could congregate once they'd returned from sea? Thinking about the Charleston she was familiar with, Belle recalled the tavern she and those aboard her ship would frequent when they arrived in port. Tomorrow she would look for it.

"Are you ready for me to show you to your room?" Susanna said.

"You're quiet as a mouse," Belle said, impressed with the woman's ability to sneak up on her.

"I don't know about that. I think you were just deep in thought."

"Perhaps."

"The harbor is beautiful, isn't it?" Susanna stood beside her gazing out over the water.

"Aye. Not what I'm used to, but beautiful nonetheless."

Susanna turned to face Belle. "I know this transition can be rough, but we're here for you."

Belle felt Susanna truly meant it. She wasn't sure she would be as kind under the circumstances. "You are kind to accommodate a stranger."

"You're a friend of Edward's. That's all I need to know." Susanna smiled a genuine smile. One that reached from her lips to her eyes and didn't waiver.

"Thank you." She wasn't sure she deserved the kindness being shown to her, but accepted it, nonetheless.

"It's my pleasure. Now, if you'll follow me." Susanna began to walk away.

Belle followed along behind her and felt an unfamiliar sense of gratitude to Susanna, Sutherland, Mackall and especially Morwenna. For the first time in months, she felt safe from capture by the English. She was in a new world where no one knew her and no one was looking for her. Tonight would be the first time in a very long time that she would sleep completely safe from harm.

* * *

Up before the sun the next morning, Belle paced the deck surprised that her hosts had not yet risen. Life in this time had made Edward soft. She was sure that would not be the case for her. Patience had never been her strong suit. Standing around waiting for others to guide her through the day wasn't going to sit well with her either, and so Belle walked to the gangplank making a split-second decision to explore Charleston on her own.

As she made her way along the dock and onto a nearby road, she was surprised at how quiet it was. The few people she passed smiled happily in her direction, but all she could seem to muster for these strangers was a scowl. In her time, it wasn't wise to drop your guard. Doing it in this time seemed even more dangerous.

Making her way through town, Belle came upon the familiar brick façade of McCrady's, the tavern from her time. It was still here and looking better than it had in days gone by. Not much had changed about the building itself, even the tavern name remained the same. She tried the large glass door, but it was locked. That was different. Where did sailors go when they arrived in port overnight? Still, despite the changes in the surrounding buildings which now housed shops and eateries, it felt good to know that some things had survived the centuries, giving her a sense of familiarity that she needed. Feeling out of place was disconcerting, but seeing the tavern, *The Dagger,* and the colorful homes she recalled from her last visit to Charleston eased her mind in the midst of all of the things she had yet to understand.

Feeling a bit more at ease, Belle headed off down the road past the shops that lined either side of the street. She took her time, gazing in the windows filled with decorations of all kinds. It was clear none were open for business yet and she would have to wait to explore inside of them. Every now and again a small carriage would pass by. She observed people seated inside as they moved down the street seemingly by magic. Each time she stopped to watch until they were out of sight and then continued on her way. The scent of the sea air no longer battled with the smell of horse manure as Belle noted the cleanliness of the streets and the lack of horses, carts or carriages. Down the street, something caught her eye. A large wooden sign with a familiar name stood out from the side of a brick building.

"It can't be. I thought he was dead." Belle blew out an uneasy breath. Perhaps he too had need of a place to hide and had somehow landed here. If so, she had business to attend to that involved the notorious Christopher Plumb.

Reaching the building she peeked through the large glass window under the sign. "What is this?" Belle couldn't believe what she was seeing. Treasure displayed under glass caught her eye. Jewels, coins and other valuables sparkled as the rising sun shone through the glass windows. She squinted hard as she glanced at a familiar object set among the many treasures. "That bastard!" The only entry was to her right. Marching to the door she took hold of the handle and pulled. It was locked.

"Does no one rise with the sun in this place?" She rattled the door, but not a sound came from within. Pacing back and forth Belle understood there was only one way to get to the treasure. Unsheathing her cutlass she used the butt end to fracture the glass. Reaching her hand in she found what must be the lock and turned it. The door opened and as it did, a loud clanging sound rattled her nerves and pounded her ears.

The loud noise would not deter her. She headed straight for the treasure under glass and once again using her cutlass, smashed through. Gold and silver coins, emerald brooches, ruby necklaces. The trove was filled with treasure of every kind and she was sure some of the pieces were those stolen from her and her father by Christopher Plumb. Filling her pockets with whatever she could, Belle felt no guilt at all. The man had stolen from her. It was only fair and right that she steal from him.

A sound from behind caught her attention. She slowly turned to find four men brandishing guns all aimed in her direction.

"Empty your pockets," the one nearest her said.

"Who are you?" she asked. She sized up the men and noted that not only were they carrying weapons, but they were also blocking the only exit.

The one obviously in charge shouted, "We're the police. Now, do as you're told."

Belle knew that alone she was no match for these men and so she emptied her pockets.

"Now, put any weapons you may have on the ground." She removed the cutlass from her boot, two flintlocks from her waistband, a dirk sheathed inside her jacket and a small palm-sized knife from up her sleeve. She couldn't help but notice the looks of disbelief on the faces of those watching her. One of them approached slowly, pulling a shiny pair of handcuffs from his belt and locked them around her wrists.

Under normal circumstances Belle would never have found herself in this predicament, but it seemed she had no choice but to obey. She would bide her time and wait for an opportune moment to escape, just as she'd done the other times she'd been detained by authorities.

"What's going on here?" A man she would have recognized anywhere entered the room.

"Christopher Plumb, you bilge sucking scurvy dog." She spat the words with venom in the direction of her sworn enemy.

"I'm sorry. Do I know you?" he asked, seeming a bit taken aback by her insult.

"Aye. You do," she snarled.

"Sir, what do you want to do here. It's obvious she broke in and was stealing from your cases."

"I was only taking what is rightfully mine," Belle said.

Christopher Plumb gazed at her as though trying to remember who she might be and how she knew him.

"Have you had all sense knocked from your head?" Belle asked. "Do you think you can steal from me and get away with it?"

"Sir. I believe we'll take her to the station. You can decide if you want to file charges once we get her booked."

"Alright," Christopher said. "I'll be along shortly. First, I have to secure the door."

"We'll leave an officer here with you. He can keep an eye on the door while you take stock of any missing treasure."

"Thank you."

The men escorted Belle out to the street where a crowd of people stood by watching them. Once she had been seated in the strangest conveyance she'd ever laid eyes on, the magical carriage moved on its own much like the small boats she'd seen the night before and the vehicles she'd observed earlier in the street.

* * *

CHRISTOPHER PLUMB WAS LEFT SCRATCHING his head. Who was this woman all dressed in pirate garb and covered from head to toe in silver coins? She said he should know her, but for the life of him he had no idea whatsoever who the woman might be.

He took quick stock of the cases and found only one item missing. It was the silver cap to a walking stick that had once belonged to the notorious pirate, John Silver. *Why would she want that?* he wondered. Double checking the broken case and the others around the room, he didn't locate the cap, which was inscribed with the initials *JS*.

"Is everything alright?" Susanna Sutherland made her way into the museum, her brow furrowed in worry. "What happened?"

"The museum was broken into." He stood there feeling confused and out of sorts.

"Did they catch him?" Susanna placed her hand on his arm.

"Her. And yes. They caught her in the act." He covered her hand with his. "I'm alright. No need to worry. I know the risk of having treasure displayed this way may bring the occasional thief, but this was a very strange situation."

"In what way?"

"Well, she was very angry with me. Saying I had stolen from her, the woman's accusations seemed so personal. As a museum curator, I have to admit I've never had anyone call me such colorful names."

"Uh oh," Susanna said, dropping her hand to her side.

"What do you mean 'uh oh'?" Christopher asked.

"What did this woman look like?"

"She was dressed like a pirate, but one all decked out in silver coins." From what he'd seen of her she was quite beautiful as well.

"Belle," Susanna said. "What happened to her? Where is she now?" She seemed particularly agitated.

"The police station. I'm heading that way now." Christopher took her hands in his, to calm her.

"I'm coming with you," Susanna said.

"I take it you know this woman. Does she work for you?" All he could imagine was that she might be one of the local crew who worked aboard *The Dagger.*

Susanna peeked at the officer guarding the door before whispering. "Belle Silver. She time traveled here last night. She was aboard

The Dagger but must have decided to explore the city without us this morning."

"I see. Belle Silver?" he asked, releasing her hands.

"Yes. John Silver's daughter. I'm sure you've heard of him."

He definitely knew who John Silver was, although he didn't know he had a daughter or that she was a pirate. He felt at a loss. He prided himself on being a pirate expert and the thought that there was something he didn't know about John Silver reminded him that there was always something new to learn about the past. "That would explain a couple of things."

"What's that?" Susanna asked.

"First, now I know why she took the only piece I have that belonged to him."

"And the other?"

"She kept accusing me of knowing her. She must have known my ancestor, Christopher Plumb."

"I'm sure she did. And Edward said you look just like him. She probably thinks you *are* him! We have to get her out of jail, Christopher." Susanna turned towards the door, seeming for all the world like she might run all the way to the police station on her own.

Christopher approached the policeman at the door. "Officer would you mind staying here while I go down to the station? I'll send the glass guy over right away to replace the door."

"No problem, sir. I'm happy to do it," the man replied.

They began walking towards the police station. "What were you doing down this way?" Christopher wondered.

"I was looking for Belle. I didn't want her to get lost or get in trouble. I guess I'm too late for that one. Edward took the other end of town."

The shops were just beginning to open. More and more people were now out and about. While Christopher was upset about his museum, he was relieved it was his place she'd broken into. Anyone else would have been sure to press charges and who knows what would have happened at that point.

"Why don't you call and have Edward meet us, while I get my glass guy on the phone."

Christopher dialed Russ, an old friend and the owner of the local glass shop. Russ assured him he would get the door taken care of immediately, as well as the broken glass case.

"Edward's on his way," Susanna said as they approached police headquarters. "I can't believe she wasn't even here a full twenty-four hours and she's already in trouble."

Christopher couldn't help but laugh. He would never have expected to be robbed by real a pirate. Having never heard of Belle Silver in all of his research on pirates from his seven times great-grandfather's day, Christopher was eager to find out more. He was also hopeful that the hatred he'd seen in those beautiful turquoise eyes would be replaced with something more serene once Belle realized he wasn't the man she thought he was.

The police station was located in a centuries old brick building that had been revamped to hold the current police station. Stairs led to large double doors and then into a lobby that contained wooden benches lined up against the walls and a large wood desk manned by several police officers and clerks. An excellent job had been done in restoring the building to its former glory while meshing it with the practicality needed to operate the police station.

As they waited at the lobby desk, Edward joined them. He had become Christopher's good friend since arriving in Charleston. They'd first met on a treasure hunting expedition and along the way Christopher had been instrumental in reuniting Edward and Susanna after they'd been separated because neither one of them wished to live in another time. Edward finally saw the light when he realized he couldn't live without Susanna and returned to Charleston for good. He admired Edward's ability to adapt to life in present day Charleston and to start a thriving business. He felt incredibly lucky to have both of them in his life.

Edward's irritation was evident as he paced back and forth. "I can't believe we're here already. I thought she'd at least take a day or two before diving right into robbery or mayhem of some sort."

"I've spoken with the sergeant. I told him I wasn't interested in pressing charges. He now officially thinks I've lost my mind."

"Thank you, Christopher. We'll have a talk with her."

"Okay. I'm going to leave before they bring her out. I'm pretty sure she wants to kill me, so I'll leave her to you. Please explain that I'm one of the good guys."

"I'll do my best," Edward said.

"Oh and tell her she can keep the cane grip that belonged to her father. She is the rightful owner." It was one of Christopher's prized pieces, but how could he deny that John Silver would have preferred his daughter to have it.

"Come by for dinner later. We'll have this all sorted out by then," Susanna said.

"I'll call first just to be on the safe side."

"Good plan," she replied.

This really was quite the puzzle, but as the owner of The Christopher Plumb Museum, a lifelong treasure hunter, and an avid collector of all things pirate, he was curious to find out what it was Belle thought had been stolen from her.

He also wanted to find out more about Belle Silver.

The walk back to the museum gave him plenty of time to think about the woman he'd seen in his shop. She was younger than him, but not by too many years. The memory of her silver coins jingling as she left the museum with the police caused an amused smile to spread across his face. He chuckled to himself. He hadn't been blind to the fact that she was very attractive. Those eyes and the way she'd looked at him were emblazoned in his mind. He hoped he could change that the next time he saw her.

CHAPTER 4

"What were you thinking?" Edward asked, seeming more annoyed with her than perhaps he'd ever been.

Belle assumed he'd understand, but apparently not since he'd already asked the question a half dozen times. The walk back to *The Dagger* was far too long under the circumstances.

"Edward, leave her alone," Susanna said. She had become a surprise ally in this matter. "She's only just arrived and she doesn't know the rules of the road, so to speak."

Belle rolled her father's silver cane grip around and around in the palm of her hands. The feel of it brought back memories of her father and how many times his hand had touched this very cane grip. It stung how much she missed him.

"I know you have hard feelings about Christopher Plumb, but this is not the Christopher Plumb you knew in the past," Edward said.

"He looks just like him," Belle replied. She was having a hard time separating the two and not just because they looked alike.

"He's the great, great, great, etc. grandson of Christopher Plumb and he just so happens to have the same name." Edward threw his hands in the air in apparent exasperation.

"All those treasures he has in his *museum,* they don't belong to him." This was the other reason. The original Plumb had broken his agreement and run off with a treasure haul that truthfully belonged to Belle and her father.

"Nor do they belong to you," Edward said. A calmness had returned to his voice encouraged by Susanna's elbow to his side.

"Some of them may be mine." Belle defended herself. "Where did he get them?"

"He's a treasure hunter," Edward explained, seeming impatient with her.

Belle snickered. "Aren't we all?"

"In a way, but in this time, he searches for treasure that he knows is out there somewhere and has never been found. His efforts helped Mackall, and the crew of *The Dagger* find a treasure we'd all been in search of for a very long time. His share of that treasure is mainly what you'll find in the museum."

"He's a really nice guy," Susanna said. "You should give him a chance. Take the time to get to know him."

Belle gave Susanna a sideways glance. She couldn't remember ever meeting any genuinely nice men and was having a hard time believing the namesake of Christopher Plumb could be one. The men of her crew were pirates. Being nice would be a death knell for them. While they were pleasant enough companions and, in some sense, the only family she'd known for many years, she wouldn't call them nice. That would be insulting to them.

"Edward we should really get Belle some new clothes." Susanna said. She glanced at Belle and explained. "So you fit in better."

"People are staring," Edward explained.

The man truly knew how to irritate her. They'd known each other many years, but thankfully had spent little time together. On the rare occasion when they did cross paths it was usually in a tavern surrounded by the men of her crew and whoever Sutherland happened to be there with. After a few ales he was much more tolerable, and she was sure he felt the same about her.

"Let them stare." Belle's defiant reply came with a stiffening of her spine and an upward tilt of her head.

"I'm just concerned that someone may try to steal your silver," Susanna said.

"I dare them to try," Belle snapped, her hand reaching to that familiar spot where she'd kept her cutlass, that is until it had been confiscated by the police along with all the other weapons she'd had hidden on her person. Everything was now in a box being carried by Edward. He told her he'd hold them for her as they weren't necessary here. She felt naked without them and taking the box from Edward removed her cutlass and flintlock pistol. She placed the flintlock in her boot and the cutlass in her waistband.

Edward rolled his eyes and shook his head at her, but Belle really didn't care what he thought. She was a pirate captain and he a lowly quartermaster.

"Please, let us buy you some new clothes." Susanna was pleading with her. "We'll get you a makeover."

She had no idea what a makeover was, but if it got them to stop bothering her she would agree. "If that is what you want."

"Yay!" Susanna clapped her hands excitedly.

All Belle could do was shake her head and follow along.

"I'm going back to the ship, you two enjoy yourselves," Edward said, holding the box of Belle's weapons close.

"We will." Susanna assured as she gave him a peck on the lips. "Come on, Belle. This is going to be fun."

Belle and Susanna spent the better part of the day shopping for clothing. Belle tried on every single thing Susanna had handed her. While Belle was busy in the small room filled with mirrors, she could hear Susanna on the phone directing people who were helping with the ship's Christmas party. Belle was impressed as she listened to her clarifying the menu with the caterer and organizing the crew who would work that night.

Susanna put the phone back in her purse. "Sorry about that. I used to own an event planning business and now I run the pirate cruise business. Edward is my partner, but he's the sailor. He handles every-thing to do with the ship and crew. I handle the advertising, the suppliers and all those pesky details that are part of running your own business."

Belle was developing a newfound respect for Susanna. She wasn't just Edward's wife. She was a woman who took charge and knew how to get things done just like Belle.

Now laden down with their many bags they were headed to a place Susanna called a blowout bar, whatever that meant. She'd made sure that Belle changed into one of the outfits they'd purchased at the last shop they visited. Belle made sure to keep her pirate garb close by her side. It wasn't hard to convince Susanna to leave it in Belle's hands as it was quite heavy and after a brief attempt at carrying the bag it was in, she was happy to hand it over to Belle. Used to wearing men's breeches made specifically for her, Belle thought the one's they'd purchased for her felt very different and lightweight. Along with the silken shirt she was wearing, it felt almost as if she wore nothing at all. A *drapey* jacket, Susanna had called it topped everything off.

Once they'd arrived, Belle was ushered to a chair that spun in circles. She gave it a try two or three times before the woman with the gun shaped object harrumphed loudly so she would sit still.

"Let's get your hair washed first," the woman said.

Leaning her back in the chair, Belle experienced the most wonderful feeling. Warm water sprayed her hair and then a soapy lather was applied. The woman massaged her scalp, relaxing Belle so much so that she audibly moaned.

"Feels good, doesn't it?" Susanna asked.

"Mmmm," Belle managed to say as another spray of warm water rinsed her hair. Another mixture was applied to her hair and massaged through before it too was rinsed off. They wrapped her head in a towel and then walked her to another chair where she sat facing herself in the mirror. Susanna's grin was large enough to take over her whole face as she stood behind them watching.

"Don't worry," Susanna said. "This is all normal." And then to the woman said, "She's never done anything like this before."

A blast of noise and hot air came out of the woman's gun as she pointed it at Belle's head. Her instinct was to duck, but she soon realized this gun was meant to dry her hair. In her wildest dreams she could never have imagined any of this.

As the woman brushed and dried her hair, Belle was mesmerized by the woman who appeared in the mirror. If she hadn't seen the change herself, she would have questioned who this beautiful woman was. Not that she didn't think herself beautiful. She'd been told many times, but this was different. Her long dark locks shined like the ocean water on a calm day. Carefully placed curls framed her face and cascaded down her shoulders and over her breasts. The woman turned off the gun and fluffed Belle's hair with her hands.

"What do you think?" she asked.

Belle looked at Susanna who said, "She looks great. Thank you so much."

"Are you going somewhere special tonight?" the woman asked.

"No," Belle said, eyeing Susanna.

"We just thought she deserved a *me* day," Susanna explained.

They paid the woman and headed back out to the busy sidewalk.

"Edward won't believe it," Susanna said.

"What do you mean?" Belle asked.

"He's probably never seen you like this."

"No, he hasn't. I've never seen me like this." Belle agreed.

"I know that was all weird for you," Susanna said. "I want you to know that I understand how you're feeling. When I traveled back to your time with Edward, I had to learn how things worked and believe me it wasn't easy being without my hair dryer and makeup. But, you know, even without all of those things, Edward still wanted to be with me. It just showed me that it wasn't all about what I looked like on the outside. He saw something in me that made him want to be a better man."

"You've done what many women wanted to do. You captured Edward Sutherland's heart."

"He captured mine," Susanna said.

"I am happy for him and for you." Belle was telling the truth. If someone like Edward Sutherland could change his ways, then perhaps she could as well. Today had been a good start. She'd changed her appearance, which would bode well for her stay here in this time, but she had one question. Smiling warmly at Susanna, she said, "Now, let me ask you this. If what you look like on the outside isn't important, then why have we spent this whole day changing the way I look?"

Susanna looked thoughtful before answering. "Good point. It doesn't make you who you are, but it does feel good to get new clothes and be pampered. Besides, it will make your stay here a little bit easier."

"Easier than your stay in my time." Belle teased. Having only ever lived her adult life as a pirate, she wasn't sure she could fit in here, but she would try. Besides, being able to disappear in a crowd was an important skill for a pirate and everyone here seemed to notice her clothing. She chuckled to herself thinking about her day.

"What's so funny?" Susanna asked.

"I cannot believe that my first day here I managed to find trouble."

"I imagine old habits die hard," Susanna said. There was a twinkle in her eyes that told Belle she was being teased.

She swatted Susanna's arm and almost sent her flying off of the sidewalk before catching her and setting her upright. "Sorry. I meant no harm."

"If that was you joking around, I'd hate to see what you'd do if you were really angry."

Belle laughed again. "There is many a man who could tell you what happens when you make Belle Silver angry."

Susanna began walking again and Belle fell in place beside her. "Let's get back to the ship. Edward will be waiting for us."

"Will he cook for us again?" Belle asked, thinking of the good food she'd had the night before.

"I think he will. We might invite Christopher to join us."

"Why would you do that?" Belle snapped. The last person she wanted to see was Christopher Plumb, especially since she had just tried to rob him. Although, she could use a treasure hunter and if he'd helped Edward find his, then he might be useful to her.

"We won't if you'd rather not, but we thought it would be good for you two to get to know each other. You'll see he's not the Christopher Plumb you knew."

"So you've said, but I'm not so sure." She was having a hard time separating the two. She had such hard feelings for the man she knew from her own time that letting go of her anger and trusting that this Christopher was not his ancestor was really throwing her off.

"Think about it. That's all we're asking."

"Why is it so important to you?" Belle asked.

"He's our very good friend and we like to get together for dinner at least once a week. it would be easier if you two got along."

Belle gave it some thought. Still wondering about all that treasure in his museum, she imagined getting to know this Christopher Plumb might be beneficial.

"I will do it for you," Belle said.

"Yes!" Susanna threw her fist in the air, causing Belle to laugh even more.

After spending the whole day with Susanna, Belle had to admit that it had been most enjoyable. She hadn't had any women friends since she was young. Truth be told, she had always been more comfortable in the company of men, finding the things that interested women to be vapid and uninspired. While they had only shopped all day, Susanna had discussed many things with her. She told her about finding *The Dagger* here in port and how she and Edward had started a business using the ship to take tourists on pirate cruises along the coast. Admittedly Susanna had only just learned about ships, but she already knew more about it than one would expect. She was smart, capable and as she told Belle, a business woman and a boss. She and Edward had carved out a lovely life for themselves here in this time. Susanna was Edward's equal in every way, and was treated with respect by everyone she worked with.

As for the other women she saw, none of them were parading around in overly large poofy dresses or powdered wigs as were common in her day. They seemed much happier in her mind as they roamed the streets unescorted and doing exactly what they pleased.

Belle had chosen piracy as a way of life in order to be a woman free from all of that. No one told her what to do. She made the rules on her ship and not one man aboard had ever questioned her.

Edward greeted them on their return. "Did you ladies enjoy yourselves?"

Belle bristled at the term ladies.

"We did," Susanna said, kissing his cheek.

"I've invited Christopher to join us tonight. I assured him that Belle was no longer interested in killing him."

"What kind of man is he who would be so fearful?" Belle asked.

"I'm only joking," Edward said. He placed an arm around Susanna's shoulders. "Come tell me all about your day." The couple walked away towards their cabin, but Edward had one more thing to say. "And by the way, you look beautiful Belle."

Not knowing how to reply was becoming a habit for Belle. She stood on deck for a moment in awe of the journey she'd taken only yesterday. She wished her father were here to enjoy it with her, but that wasn't possible. Although he had always wanted better for her, Belle fought him every step of the way until he gave in and accepted her as a pirate aboard his ship. He'd taught her everything she needed to survive in that world and perhaps in this. An uncharacteristic tear slid down her cheek as she looked to the heavens and whispered, "I miss you, father."

Once in her cabin, she plunked herself down on the edge of her bed. The bags she'd been carrying lay strewn at her feet. Looking in the full-length mirror on the bathroom door, she didn't recognize the woman she saw. Could she be a woman in this time and still be all of the things she wanted to be? Opening the bag that contained her own clothing, she set them out on the bed. Black leather leggings and jacket laid upon the coverlet as though they contained a person. Belle still wore her boots. She refused to part with them for the shoes Susanna had chosen for her. Susanna bought them anyway, but Belle doubted she would ever wear them. She placed her belt, hat and linen shirt where they would go when she wore them next and stared down at them. Belle would wear them again. They reminded her she was a pirate and they reminded her of where she'd come from. They told her Belle would not be left behind or forgotten. It was a promise she was making to herself and one she would keep.

CHAPTER 5

Christopher planned his arrival at *The Dagger* for precisely seven that evening. He was both apprehensive and excited to officially meet Belle Silver. When he'd phoned Susanna earlier, she told him they had everything under control and that Belle had agreed to have dinner with them. It was a start. Christopher knew there had been women pirates, Anne Bonny, Grace O'Malley and Mary Read were a few that came to mind. Why he'd never heard of Belle Silver baffled him. He considered himself an expert on pirate history and read everything he could about Golden Age pirates. Still, he wasn't smug enough to think there weren't new things to learn. He hoped that like Edward Sutherland, Belle Silver could add to his knowledge of the era.

He sauntered along enjoying the Christmas decorations that were sprouting up all around Charleston. Many boats docked in the marina were already decorated with trees, lights and large wooden cutouts of Santa Claus, snowmen and reindeer. They were getting ready for the annual holiday boat parade. This was by far his favorite time of year. It always had been. His mother and father always went all out decorating their home and participating in a neighborhood tradition of

Christmas caroling and potlucks held at his parents' home as well as neighboring households.

Christopher inhaled deeply, enjoying the scent of the ocean mixed with the aromas of delicious food emanating from each restaurant he passed. He wondered what Edward would be serving them tonight but knew that whatever it was it would be just as delicious as anything from a five-star eatery.

Surrounded by many smaller vessels, *The Dagger* loomed large as he got closer. He'd promised Susanna he would help with decorations and in turn she told him she would help decorate the museum. Thankfully the door had been replaced that afternoon and so it was one less thing for him to worry about.

"Christopher!" Susanna called from the rail of the ship.

He waved up to her and picked up the pace. Susanna had become a good friend and one he couldn't imagine his life without. As he stepped onto the main deck, she greeted him with a quick hug and a peck on the cheek.

"Wait until you see Belle." Susanna said, seeming quite excited.

"Why? What have you done to her?" he chuckled, knowing Susanna would have been eager to transform her into a modern-day woman.

"You'll see." She hooked her arm through his and led him down to the galley.

"Something smells delicious," Christopher said.

"Christopher, I'm so glad you came." Edward stirred a large pot before placing a lid over it.

"Susanna assured me that I didn't have to fear for my life, so here I am."

"Very funny," Edward replied.

"Where is she?" Christopher asked.

"I'm here," Belle stood so close behind Christopher that when he turned, he almost knocked into her.

He couldn't believe his eyes. Belle looked nothing like the pirate who had been arrested earlier that day.

"Have you nothing to say?" she asked.

"Of course. Good to see you again." He held out his hand to shake hers, but she didn't reciprocate. "How was your day?" That was a stupid thing to ask. "I mean…not your morning, obviously, but the rest of the day." He stammered his way through, hoping he didn't sound too idiotic.

"It was very nice. Susanna is a very good hostess." Belle was saying all the polite things, but her voice sounded less than friendly.

"Shall we all sit up on deck? I'll bring the cocktails," Edward said.

"Yes. Let's do that," Susanna said, leading the way up the stairs to the main deck.

Christopher waited for the women to sit and then took his own seat in one of the cushioned chairs that had been set in a circle around a drink table that also held a small firepit, the flames of which served to warm the immediate area while adding a romantic ambiance. An awkward silence ensued as they sat and stared into the fire.

Edward appeared with a tray of drinks. Christopher hoped it would lead to more and easier conversation. Actually, any conversation at all would be a relief. When it was just Edward, Susanna and him, conversation flowed without effort. This new dynamic was going to be interesting.

"You've traveled through time," Christopher said, stating the obvious.

"I have," Belle answered.

He might as well get it out of the way now and hope that the evening would be peaceful. "I'm not the Christopher Plumb that you knew. He was my many times great-grandfather. I hope that any dealings you may have had with him won't keep us from being friends." There he'd said his piece. The rest was up to her.

Belle's eyes narrowed a bit and Christopher was prepared for her anger to erupt, but to his surprise, her gaze softened just enough that he didn't feel his life was in imminent danger.

"I'm curious," she said. "How did you find the treasure you display in your museum?"

Unsure of what she'd been about to say, Christopher let go of the breath he'd been holding when she began to speak. "I've been hunting treasure for years. Most of what you see in the museum was shared with me by the crew of *The Dagger*."

"Edward said as much." Belle replied.

Feeling nervous, Christopher wondered where Edward was with those drinks. He thought if he just kept talking about the thing that interested Belle the most, then all would be well. "I had been searching for the very same treasure, but even though I was digging in the right spot, I found nothing. Edward took that information back with him to his own time and much to everyone's delight, there it was."

"Do you do this treasure hunting on your own?" Belle leaned forward in her chair, focusing all of her attention on him.

In response, Christopher sat back surprised that despite the calm of her words she still seemed angry with him. "I do. I have lots of equipment to help me though."

Edward handed each of them a glass. Tonight they would be drinking Hurricanes it seemed. Christopher would have to pace himself. He wasn't much of a drinker, so he sipped his. "Very good, Edward."

"Thank you. I've been practicing. Those moonlight cruises we do require that I know how to make many different drinks."

Belle made a face. She examined her glass and the tiny umbrella Edward had placed in it. She eyed her host with a look of disbelief. "Do you not have rum?"

"It's in the drink. Two kinds I might add."

"Would you prefer something less fruity?" Christopher offered.

"I would." She set her glass down, pushing it as far away from herself as possible.

"I'll get it, Edward. Be right back."

Christopher was feeling uncomfortable. Belle hadn't taken her eyes off him since they'd sat down. It would be different if the look she was giving him was anything but an angry glare. Perhaps if she saw that he meant her no harm the tension would ease between them.

He found a bottle of rum and a glass, which he brought back up on deck.

"Here you go." He opened the bottle and poured for her.

"Thank you." She accepted the glass, taking a large drink before setting it down.

"Did you get your door fixed?" Susanna asked.

"Russ came by right away and took care of it." Christopher glanced at Belle, who was looking past them at something off in the distance. "No hard feelings by the way."

"Christopher Plumb was not a good man. He took what was not his to take."

"Isn't that the definition of piracy?" Christopher asked.

Belle seemed irritated by this statement. "Yes, we take from others, but it is frowned upon to take from your brethren."

"Well said. Again, I am not that Christopher Plumb. I am not a pirate." Why did he feel the need to keep repeating himself?

"No. You are not, but yet you have a trove of treasure that undoubtedly does not belong to you." Belle eyed him over the rim of her glass.

Susanna and Edward exchanged glances that said they didn't like where this conversation was leading.

Christopher looked directly into Belle's turquoise blue eyes wanting her to know he was serious and for a moment was lost there. "Why don't you come by the museum tomorrow and take a look at what I have there? I can tell you where I acquired every piece and if you see anything that belongs to you, I am happy to part with it."

"That's very generous of you." Belle's voice was low and sultry to his ears.

"Belle that's not an invitation to clear out the museum, do you understand?" Edward warned.

Susanna elbowed her husband and gave him an I-can't-believe-you-said-that look.

"Why would you think I would do that?" Belle asked.

"You're a pirate, remember?"

"How could I forget." She chuckled and the blue of her eyes became less icy when she gazed at Christopher.

* * *

AFTER A DELICIOUS MEAL, Belle found herself alone on deck with Christopher while Edward and Susanna cleaned up. The Edward she knew would never have participated in such domestic tasks. Susanna, it seemed, had tamed him.

"Gorgeous, isn't it?" Christopher said, breaking the silence.

"Aye."

"I never take for granted the fact that I get to live in such a beautiful place. It's always a sight to see, but at Christmas time it takes on an enchanted feeling."

"How so?" Belle asked. If she kept him talking, she wouldn't have to say much. She preferred it that way.

"In so many ways. People are friendlier, the decorations are the best and I love the Christmas carols that play everywhere." He glanced her way, but she kept her eyes looking straight ahead. "Do you like Christmas?"

"I've never really given it much thought." That was a lie, but it rolled easily off her tongue. She had loved Christmas as a child. The fancy treats and small gifts she received lived on in her memories. On the other hand, Christmas aboard a pirate ship took on a whole new meaning.

"Don't you celebrate?" Christopher asked.

Damn the man, he kept asking questions that she felt she had to answer. Belle knew Susanna and Edward valued Christopher's friendship, but she didn't need a friend and she certainly didn't trust him. She wasn't about to let her guard down, but he might be useful to her in the search for her father's treasure. She turned to face him. He was a handsome man, though she had never thought that about his ancestor. His graying hair did not make him appear old. His dark eyes were filled with curiosity and a softness she wasn't used to. They crinkled in the corners as he smiled warmly at her. "I've had little reason to celebrate of late."

"I'm sorry to hear that."

She imagined he truly was. "Don't be sorry. I have not missed it."

"While you're here, let me show you how we celebrate in Charleston."

Why was he being so pleasant with her? Was there something wrong with him? Or was he trying to manipulate her the way she was trying to manipulate him into helping her. He seemed so earnest though. Had she been a pirate so long that she was unable to recognize a genuine, heartfelt interest being shown to her? She looked into his eyes and for a moment felt herself being drawn into his web, like a spider with a fly. She quickly looked away, feeling confused and thrown off course. This would not do.

Susanna and Edward appeared. As they approached, Edward said with a chuckle, "Good. He still has all his fingers and his ears are still attached to his head."

"Edward!" Susanna playfully swatted at his arm. "How are you two getting along?"

"We're fine," Christopher replied. "I was just telling Belle about the wonders of Christmas in Charleston."

"I'm excited about that, too," Susanna said. "I haven't been here that long, so I'm sure there are events I'm not aware of."

"I'd be happy to take you to some of them," Christopher said. "I've already told Belle I'd love to show her around town."

"That's a great idea. Don't you agree?" Susanna directed this to Belle.

"Aye." She was stuck now. She would have to discover the wonders of Charleston while all she really wanted was to find her father's treasure.

"It's getting late and I really should get going. Belle, I'll expect you at the museum in the morning. Maybe not as early as today." Christopher's smile lit his face. His eyes twinkled and when he reached out a hand to touch Belle's arm, she felt she would melt from the heat of it. Something about this man was speaking to her in a way no one else had before.

The corners of her lips turned up in a slight smile. She wanted to like this man, but suspicion and mistrust ran deep in her veins. There was no telling whether or not he could break through those barriers.

"Good night," she managed to say. It felt odd being nice and polite. Pirates were anything but polite when they were together.

"Good night, all," Christopher said as he his way down the gangplank.

When he was out of sight, Belle felt a sudden urge to lie down. This whole day had been exhausting. "Good night." Not waiting for a reply, Belle left the main deck for her cabin where she spent the better part of the night thinking about Christopher Plumb, the strange pull she felt towards him, and how odd it was that he was a descendant of a man she found reprehensible under the best of circumstances.

CHAPTER 6

Detective Joe Manning stood on the sidewalk outside of the police station alongside Dan Hunt, a local private detective.

"Did you see that weird woman who was arrested this morning?" Hunt asked.

"I questioned her when she came in," Manning said. He'd been on the force for well over twenty years and was seriously considering retirement. Today, he thought it might actually be possible to retire with enough money to last the rest of his life.

"What's with that outfit? It must be worth a small fortune." Hunt was nothing if not inquisitive about absolutely everything. It's what made him a good detective.

"Yeah. Lots of silver coins. They looked like Spanish pieces of eight." Manning had been fascinated with the woman. As a police detective he saw all kinds of people. Every day it was something new and sometimes unbelievable, but this woman was intriguing. There was something about her that seemed dangerous. It could have been the cache of weapons on her, but he sensed it was something else altogether.

"Wonder where she got them?" Hunt asked.

"Probably a treasure hunter, is my guess." Manning carefully removed a folded piece of paper from his pocket and motioned for Hunt to come closer. He glanced around to make sure no one was close enough to see what they were up to. "I made two copies of the original before I gave it back to her. One for you and one for me."

"What is it?" Hunt took the paper from his hand, examining it. His eyebrows shot up as he looked to Manning for an explanation.

"Looks like a treasure map." Manning retrieved the map, folded it and then handed it back to Hunt. "Put that away and don't let anyone else know you have it. Understood?" While he trusted Hunt, he wanted to be sure he knew it wasn't to be passed around.

"Is it real?" Hunt's voice rose in anticipation.

"I don't know. I'm going to do some research. If it is, I think we should try to locate it, don't you?" Manning couldn't help but smile. He had a good feeling about this. A very good feeling.

"Hell yeah," Hunt said.

"I'll let you know what I find out." Manning hoped it would be the answer to his prayers for early retirement.

Manning and Hunt were around the same age and had known each other ever since their time at the police academy. Manning had graduated, but Hunt didn't and chose to be a private detective instead. As he told Manning, he preferred to be his own boss. They'd maintained a friendship over the years. Women had come and gone, but their relationship had lasted the test of time. On a professional level, when Manning needed help with a case, Hunt was his man. He knew he could trust him to do the work and if anything happened to fall into their laps, Hunt was always eager to join in. He often had leads on things that were happening in the Charleston area that the police were unaware of. What the higher ups didn't know, wouldn't hurt them. Adventure was something they both craved, especially one that could net them millions of dollars each.

They'd done some jobs in the past that were outside of the bounds of what one might consider legal, but they hadn't been caught and so they were always looking for that next big payoff. It would be good to get back in the game, especially if this time they could come out big winners.

Rubbing his hands together, Hunt's excitement was palpable. "I'm excited. Hurry up and figure it out."

"Maybe we'll make some extra cash for Christmas presents."

"Christmas presents? I could use a new car or boat." Hunt seemed overjoyed at the prospect.

"Don't get your hopes up. It might be nothing. In the meantime, can you tail her? We wouldn't want to be late to the party, now would we?"

"Sure. I'll keep an eye on her." Hunt stroked his chin and nodded to two patrolmen leaving the station. "I'm curious though. Why didn't Plumb press charges? Do you think he knows her?"

"Could be? If he does, I'll find out soon enough."

"He's a treasure hunter, if I remember correctly. Maybe they're in it together." Manning tried to put the pieces of the puzzle together, but had more questions than answers. He hoped Hunt would have more luck. "Still, why did she try to rob him?"

"Maybe she was mad about something," Hunt said. "You know how women are."

"I suppose that's possible." Manning understood where Hunt was coming from. The man's wife had caught him cheating and had taken him for everything he had. House, car, and money. "The other odd thing was the number of weapons she had on her."

"Really?" Hunt's ears perked up on hearing this.

"Yeah. They were all antiques. Knives mostly, but a couple of flint-lock pistols." Manning remembered seeing them and thinking they looked brand new. He was surprised when he examined them further and found they were at least a couple of hundred years old.

"Interesting. I'm going to enjoy this case and I have a good feeling about it too. I think we could end up very rich."

"From your mouth to God's ears," Manning said.

"Like I said, keep an eye on her. She might do us a favor and lead us right to this treasure."

Hunt laughed. "Maybe she'll even dig it up for us." He checked his watch. "You interested in getting a drink?"

"I think you've got a job to do. You should probably get started. She's staying aboard *The Dagger*."

CHAPTER 7

orning was Christopher's favorite time of day at the museum. It was as quiet inside as it was on the street outside. At this early hour few people were out and about, especially on a Sunday. Christopher let himself in and awaited Belle's arrival. It was apparent she was an early riser and since he had no desire to replace another door, he'd arrived a bit earlier than usual. The scent of freshly brewed coffee wafted through the museum as he tidied up around the place before setting out the croissants he'd picked up on his way in.

The floor mop had barely been placed back in the closet when the bell above the door jingled and he looked up to see Belle. She really was a beautiful woman. Rays of sunshine beamed around her giving her an uncharacteristic angelic appearance. An involuntary smile curled his lips as he took a moment to appreciate what he was seeing. The fact that Belle was a pirate and a time traveler intrigued him as did her heavenly appearance. "Good morning."

"Good morning," Belle replied.

His smile went from admiring to welcoming as he hoped to make her comfortable in his world. "I made us some coffee. How do you take yours?"

Her brow scrunched into a frown. "What do you mean?"

"Cream and sugar?" he asked, pointing to them.

She acknowledged him with a nod. "Aye."

He turned his back to her while he got the coffee ready. Placing it in one of the museum mugs he sold in his small gift shop, he hoped he could trust her. It was his nature to trust people and even though he had reason enough not to, he was determined to give her the benefit of the doubt.

"Here you go." Christopher turned to hand her the mug and found that she was already examining his treasure collection.

Belle turned and walked back to him, extending her hand to accept the mug. "Thank you."

"You're welcome. Croissant?" He reached for the plate holding them. "Chocolate, Almond or plain," he said as he pointed them out to her.

Examining them closely, she chose the chocolate.

"I thought you might go for that one." Placing the croissant on a plate, Christopher grabbed a napkin and handed it to her. "Feel free to rest them on the glass cases."

Belle set the plate down before taking a sip of the coffee.

"I hope it's not too strong." Sipping from his own mug, he thought it was just right, but trying to make a good impression was making him nervous.

"It's good," Belle said. "You are a kind man. You wouldn't last long among the pirates of my crew."

Christopher froze for a moment then grinned, "I'll take that as a compliment."

"It was meant as such."

"Shall we look at some treasure?" Christopher opened the first glass case. "Most of the items in here are things I found along the Florida Gold Coast. I take my metal detector and walk along the beach. I've been lucky enough to find at least one item each time I search."

The case contained gold and silver coins, rings with emerald and ruby stones, a large silver cross and some items that appeared to be handmade nails and round lead balls used as ammunition in firearms.

"What is a metal detector?" Belle wondered. She sipped her coffee and broke off the tip of her croissant.

"I'll show you." Christopher opened the door to a small room where he kept most of his treasure hunting equipment and stepped inside. He quickly located the metal detector and brought it out to her. "Here it is."

Belle was holding some of the silver coins in her hand. "I wasn't stealing them."

Christopher chuckled. "I didn't think you were. I invited you to see if there was anything you thought might be yours. If you've found something let me know."

She placed the coins back in the case. "I haven't yet."

"This is the metal detector." He held it out to her, eager to see her reaction.

Belle took it from him. "How does it work?"

"I'll show you. Put some of those coins down on the floor for me if you would."

Belle did as he'd asked.

"Once you turn it on, you walk along holding it just above the ground like this." He walked around the room, purposely avoiding the coins. "When it scans over something metal it makes a sound." He waved it over the coins and it went nuts. "There are distinct sounds for silver and gold and one for things like lead."

"Fascinating," Belle said, eyeing the detector. "It can find things under the ground?"

"Definitely. I have other tools that I use as well. It depends on how deep I think an object might be. This metal detector can detect items about twelve inches underground. I have another that can detect much deeper."

"Interesting." Her eyes showed interest as he held the detector in his hand, but it seemed she might be holding back on showing any excitement. Perhaps she didn't wish to appear too eager.

Christopher offered it to Belle and she took it from him, seeming to test the weight of it in her hand.

"Where can I get one of these?" Belle asked, carefully examining the object from top to bottom. She lifted and turned it so she could see the bottom before setting it back down.

"No need to buy one. You can use mine. I'll take you to one of my favorite spots to try it out, if you like."

"I'd like that," she said, avoiding his gaze.

"Great. When would you like to go?" Christopher could hardly contain his excitement. He reminded himself that Belle was a pirate and that she may have a totally different reason for wishing to go with him. He on the other hand was very interested to spend some time with her doing what he loved, hunting for hidden treasure.

"Now." Belle was short and to the point.

Christopher chuckled, despite being dismayed by her brief responses. He hoped that once they were out and engaged in the search that she would be more forthcoming with him. "I'd have to get someone to watch the museum for me."

Belle looked at him expectantly.

"Maybe Susanna is available. Let me call her." He pulled his phone out of his pocket and dialed.

"What does that do?" Belle asked, pointing to his phone. "Everyone in this time seems to have one."

He held up a finger as Susanna answered. "Hey, Susanna. It's me. I was wondering if it would be possible for you to watch the museum for me. Belle would like to test out the metal detector."

"Of course. Let me finish up my paperwork and I'll be right over."

"Thanks. I'll see you in a while then."

"Will do." Susanna hung up and Christopher returned his attention to Belle.

"It allows you to speak to someone who is not here," Belle said, pointing at the phone.

"Yes. It's called a phone. It's very useful for many reasons." He held it out to her and she quietly examined it.

"When I go back to my own time I would like to take these with me." Her matter-of fact tone as she pointed to the metal detector and the phone left little room for argument.

"They wouldn't work in your time." He regretted having to disappoint her. She seemed so pleased with everything he'd been showing her.

"Why not?" Her suspicion of him seemed to have returned as her expression grew serious and her eyes narrowed.

"Several reasons, but there's nothing stopping you from using them while you're here." It would be difficult to explain the way that electronic equipment worked, but perhaps after she'd been here a while and learned about electricity and computers it would be easier. Belle seemed disappointed.

"Susanna will be here soon. Then we'll be off in search of treasure."

She took another bite of croissant. "This is chocolate?" She seemed surprised.

Christopher realized she'd probably never had chocolate in quite that form before. "It is." Her wonder was obvious in her arching brows and wide smile. It was the first sign of excitement he'd seen in her this morning. If only he'd known that all it would take was chocolate, he would have skipped the metal detector altogether and settled on breakfast for two.

"When you told me it was chocolate, this is not what I expected. I've only ever had it as a drink." She examined the croissant's innards, touching the chocolate with the tip of her tongue.

"I don't believe it was made into chocolate bars until the nineteenth century." he explained. "Do you like it?"

"Very much," she said taking another bite.

Christopher was pleased. He was enjoying the fact that she was experiencing things that were new to her and that he was the one to share them.

They looked through the rest of the cases and, much to his relief, she didn't find anything that she thought was hers. If she had, he would have gladly handed it over. He would never want to take something that rightfully belonged to another. Still he was happy his display cases remained intact and that she hadn't tried to lie to him.

Other than Christopher Plumb's treasure, which she had spent a good amount of time examining, everything else in the museum had been found along the coastal waterways.

"I'm sorry you didn't find anything," Christopher said. "Perhaps Pirate Plumb had another treasure stashed away somewhere."

"I'm sure he did." Belle stared down into one of the cases. "I see many things I would like to have, but they are yours so I will leave them with you."

"I appreciate that. I'll tell you what. If we find anything good today, it's yours to keep."

A half smile appeared as one corner of her lips curled and a sweet dimple appeared in her cheek. "If I find it, it *is* mine."

Christopher got the impression she was teasing him, but he didn't know her well enough yet to be sure. He was looking forward to this small adventure with her and to anything new he might learn about Belle Silver.

* * *

BELLE WAS SOMEWHAT disappointed that none of Christopher Plumb's treasure contained the items that had been stolen from her and her father. Perhaps Christopher was right and his ancestor had hidden it in a place where it had not yet been found. Or perhaps *this* Christopher Plumb had it hidden it away somewhere out of her sight. The map she held was her father's. He had worked aboard Plumb's vessel for a short time before earning his own ship and reaping the benefits of the many ships he'd plundered. Christopher had everything she needed to find her father's treasure, but could he be trusted to help her locate it? The thought ran around and around in her brain as she watched him get all of his equipment together. It seemed her best chance of finding John Silver's treasure was here in this time and with this equipment, although in the past she'd successfully found other treasure without benefit of a metal detector. She didn't need it, but it would certainly make the search much easier.

"Sorry it took me so long," Susanna said as she entered the museum.

"You look lovely this morning," Christopher said. "I hope I didn't interrupt any plans."

"Not at all. Edward and I don't have any plans until later. What time do you think you'll be back?"

"Probably before dinner time."

"I'm sorry. What did you say?" Belle had been watching Christopher and wondering how their day would go rather than listening to Susanna.

"Dinner tonight? Christmas trees?" Susanna asked.

Belle glanced at Christopher who nodded his head. "Yes, of course," she said.

"Well, I'll be right here when you get back. We can go together to meet Edward then. I brought my computer, so I'll keep myself busy between visitors."

"I'll put these things in the car," Christopher said, grabbing a large bag and one of his metal detectors.

"Looks as though you've got a fun day ahead of you," Susanna said.

"Fun? I think not. We're searching for treasure," Belle reminded her.

"And that's not fun?"

"'Tis work."

Susanna cocked her head and raised an eyebrow. "Okay, then don't *work* too hard."

"How will we find treasure if we don't work hard?" Belle was quite sure Susanna had never gone treasure hunting or she would know this.

Susanna held out Belle's leather breeches, jacket and linen shirt. "I thought you might want these. I thought they'd be a lot more comfortable." With her help Belle had removed the silver coins, making the plain leather outfit safer in the opinion of Susanna and Edward.

"I believe I *would* like to change," Belle took the clothing from Susanna who pointed her in the direction of the room where Christopher kept his treasure hunting tools. It had barely been a whole day, but she had missed the familiar weight of her own clothes. While people in the street had commented on her costume, it was the modern clothes that made her feel like she was putting on an act.

"Are you ready to go?" Christopher said before looking up at Belle. "Whoa! I've got to say while the clothes you had on looked great on you, I much prefer you in this." A broad smile beamed from his face.

Belle wasn't sure what to say. His words and the look in his eyes were having an unusual effect on her. She wasn't sure how to react and so she settled on a scowl.

Christopher cleared his throat and appearing somewhat embarrassed, he picked up the last of the equipment. "Ready?"

"Aye."

He headed for the door. "We'll see you later Susanna, and thank you again for helping out."

"You're welcome. Enjoy your day." Susanna followed them to the door, holding it open for them as they departed.

Belle acknowledged Susanna as she passed her and followed Christopher to his *car*, as he called it.

"Susanna has some unusual thoughts about treasure hunting," Belle said.

Christopher opened the door for her. She got into the magical vehicle while Christopher walked around and got in the other side.

"What do you mean?" he asked, fastening a strap across his chest and motioning that she should do the same.

"She seems to think we'll have fun today." Belle examined the metal piece on the end of the strap before doing what she'd seen Christopher do.

"It *will* be fun. Treasure hunting is a serious business, but it can be enjoyable even if you find nothing."

Belle harrumphed at this. She was more interested in the car and everything in it. She ran her hands over the smooth seat. There was a strange noise that drew her attention back to Christopher and his hands.

"What is that?"

"This is the steering wheel," he explained. "Much like the ship's wheel, I use this to turn the car in the direction I want to go. The sound you hear is the engine running." He turned to face her. "We had to teach Edward all about this when he first arrived. I know everything is new and strange to you, but I'm happy to answer any questions you may have."

"How do you control the speed? On the ship we use the sails." She was watching everything he did and noted his feet were placed on something near the floor.

"These pedals." Christopher pointed exactly where she'd been looking. "One is the gas, which makes it go. The harder I press, the faster we go. The other is the brake, which slows down and stops the car."

Belle nodded her head in understanding. "You are a patient man." She felt the way she had her first time aboard her father's ship. Everything had been so new to her and it took time to learn how it all worked. Some of the crew weren't interested in answering her questions, but those that took the time to teach her were her favorites.

He chuckled at this. "I'd like to think I am."

Belle observed him as he set the car in motion. He handled it with a sureness that reminded her of how she handled her ship. There was something about this man that appealed to her. He was unlike any man she'd ever met before. He was handsome, intelligent, sure of himself and he smiled often. It made her a bit suspicious at first. When a pirate smiled at you, it meant one of two things—he was either ready to steal from you or planning your death. Christopher's smile was nothing like that. It seemed genuine and warm. She felt special when he gazed at her. He was not rough and tumble like the pirates she'd known and despite the fact that he wasn't, she felt safe with him. He would guide her through this new world she found herself in and she may even learn a thing or two from him as well.

"A friend of mine owns some property just outside of town. He's given me permission to search on his land, so that's where we're headed today." He quickly glanced her way. "Is everything alright?"

She had been staring at him and became a bit self-conscious when he noticed. "Aye. Must you share your treasure with your friend?"

"Only if I find something amazing. Coins and things of that nature are of no interest to him."

Belle gazed out the window. It wouldn't do for him to find her staring at him once again and so instead she busied herself with the passing scenery.

She would point things out that were of interest to her and he would explain what they were. She enjoyed the sound of his voice and the patient tone he took as he talked to her about the road they were on and what it was paved with. There was no doubt he was quite knowledgeable, but even in his explanations he never once made her feel that he was smarter than her. He understood that because she was from a different time, some of these things would be new to her. Belle was surprised at how easy it was for her to relax in Christopher's presence. It was unusual for her to let her guard down after only knowing someone for such a short period of time. He, however, made it easy for her to *enjoy* the prospect of this treasure hunt they were on.

CHAPTER 8

*H*aving Belle beside him made today's adventure more exciting than usual. Treasure hunting was normally a solitary endeavor and one he enjoyed for that very reason. Being alone with his own thoughts had never been an issue for him. He took the time to really focus on the treasure he was seeking and the history behind it. Finding pieces that were less than one hundred years old held little interest for him, but he would take them back to the shop and keep them in a special case that he called his lost and found. No one ever appeared to claim any of it, but on the off chance they did, he'd be happy to return it to them.

A sideways glance told him he was being observed as he had been throughout the drive to Owen's Landing. Knowing she'd been watching him, he wondered what she must be thinking. If he wasn't driving he might have taken the opportunity to do the same.

From what he had been able to observe, Christopher knew she was very different from Susanna. While Susanna's nature was to be sweet and gentle, Belle was made of harder stuff, or so it seemed. He imagined in her line of work it wouldn't be beneficial to be anything but tough as nails. Once he got to know her better, it was possible Belle would let down her guard and surprise him. Maybe if he knew more about her background it would help, but somehow he didn't think she'd be willing to divulge much information. Of course, he wouldn't know unless he tried.

"Belle, tell me more about your background. I'd love to hear about you and your father."

He wasn't surprised when she frowned at him with narrowed, suspicious eyes. "Why?"

"Because I don't know you and I'd like to." He could see this wasn't going to be easy. She was still frowning.

"I'll go first. I grew up here in South Carolina. I've always lived in the Charleston area. My family has been here since the mid-eighteenth century." Christopher took the exit ramp to his friend's property before continuing. "I have a degree in archaeology, but found that I didn't enjoy traveling around the world as much as I enjoyed being here. I can look for artifacts and treasure here more easily than I can anywhere else in the world. Don't think I haven't given it a try though. When I first graduated from college, one of my professors was heading to Europe to dig for artifacts at several sites and asked me to join them. We traveled to England, France, Spain and Italy." Her face was turned away so he couldn't tell if she was even listening to him, but in case she was he thought it best to keep going. "The work was all consuming, which was fine, but I was homesick the whole time. So I came back to Charleston. I missed my friends and family. But ever since then I've specialized in pirates and the treasures from The Golden Age ever since. When Edward and Susanna brought me my relative's treasure, I decided I would open the museum to display what was found." A quick peek at his passenger told him she was no longer frowning, but she also didn't appear that interested. "Boring stuff, I know."

"Not boring," she said. "You are different, Christopher."

She had been listening. It felt good to know that he was making a connection. It was a small win, but he would take it. "I suppose I am." He wondered if that was a good thing coming from Belle. He knew he was not the average guy in that regard. He was more of what people would call a nerd, but he always had been, even as a child. Curiosity was the basis for nearly everything he did. He could see her looking at him from the corner of his eye and so he had to ask, "Is there no one like me in your time period?"

"There are those who are like you, men of knowledge and learning, but I've spent little time with them."

"Why is that?" Christopher asked.

She surprised him with a soft chuckle. "There aren't many sailing with the pirate fleets." Belle wasn't saying that there weren't knowledgeable pirates. There were many, but they'd chosen a different path, one less scholarly.

They pulled onto a gravel drive that led towards a large white farmhouse. "My friend, Matthew, is away on vacation, so we don't need to check in with him. We'll park the car here and hike to the spot I want to search."

"You've been here before," she stated.

"Many times. I keep a log of what I've found here and a chart with potential search sites. I'm fairly sure this used to be a boat landing during the Revolutionary War. It's just a creek now, so it's hard to tell unless we can find some evidence." He pulled his map out from his jacket pocket and showed it to her. Pointing to a spot near a small creek that ran through the property. "This is where we're going today. It's not far."

Getting out of the car, he waited for Belle to join him at the trunk. He took out two metal detectors. Handing one to her he then retrieved the large backpack he'd brought along. "I've got food and water in here for us."

"You've mentioned this Revolutionary War before. What happened?" she asked.

He was surprised by her interest, but happy to find a topic to continue chatting about. "In the late seventeen hundreds, the colonists revolted against England. There was a war, which the colonists won—creating the United States."

He chuckled, noting the huge grin that had now spread across her face.

"I take it you approve?" he asked.

"More than you know."

Belle followed him as he began walking away from the car. The trek to the site wouldn't take long and as they walked, Christopher took a moment to explain the topography to Belle. "Over the years, the flow of the creek has likely changed, especially because a dam was built upstream. The banks of the creek may be different than they were back two or three hundred years ago."

"I hadn't thought about that," Belle said. "So it's possible that buried treasure may be underwater or on dry land depending on how much the surrounding area has changed."

"That's exactly right. We'll see today how that may have affected this creek."

Once they were on the banks of the creek, Christopher set his backpack on an overturned tree trunk and got his detector ready. He then did the same for Belle, showing her how to use it before he began scanning the ground. She followed along beside him.

"We'll get the banks first before we head into the creek. Luckily it's not very deep right now, which will make it easier if we have to dig anything up."

Belle's detector went off almost right away. "What do I do?"

"Pinpoint the spot," Christopher replied.

Doing as he said, she stopped moving the detector in the spot where it had sounded off. "Right here. What do you think it is?"

"Let's find out." Christopher took the shovel he'd slung over his shoulder and dug into the soft ground. Setting the dirt to the side, he got out his pinpoint detector and checked the small pile. Nothing. He checked the hole and the alarm let him know that it was still in there. He dug a little deeper and repeated checking with the pinpoint detector. "Ah, it's here." Picking up the dirt in his hand he examined it and found an old button.

"What is it?" Belle asked, peering over his shoulder.

"A metal button. Probably from a uniform. Looks like from a British soldier in the eighteenth century." He handed it to Belle.

"What good is this?" she asked, as she rolled it around in her palm.

"It may not be worth a lot, but it adds to the story. We now know that at some point, either before or during the Revolutionary War there were British soldiers in this area. It may have been a campsite, or they may have just been passing through."

"No gold or silver?" Belle sounded disappointed.

"There could be. It's called a treasure hunt for a reason. There aren't any guarantees that you'll find anything at all."

Belle grumbled under her breath, obviously not thrilled with his answer.

"Do you find treasure every time you go in search of it?" he asked. Christopher was certain she didn't, but he was making a point that he hoped she would understand.

"I do not," she said. "It doesn't mean that I don't expect to."

"Patience is the key with this type of hunt. Some days I find nothing and other days I land in a spot with more than I thought possible. I don't have a treasure map to guide me."

"I do," she said. Her voice was so soft he wasn't sure she was even speaking to him.

"What?" Did he hear her correctly. This was big. Did she really trust him enough to share that information with him? He hoped she did and that he wasn't misunderstanding her.

"I have a map." She said it loud enough for him to hear clearly this time.

"With you? May I see it?" He couldn't hide his excitement on hearing this news.

Belle hesitated. Maybe she wasn't sure she could trust him yet.

"It's okay. You don't have to show me. May I ask whose treasure it is?" Christopher wanted to reassure her that he wouldn't push for any information she wasn't ready to share.

"My father's. He left me the map when he died." Her voice grew somber and she quickly looked away as he thought he saw tears well up in her eyes.

He wanted to console her, but he could see she was too proud to allow that. "I'm sorry." He handed her a hankie from his pocket. "Here. To wipe your eyes. I'm sorry if this has upset you."

"Why? Do you think that because I am a pirate I have no feelings?"

She paused, obviously gathering herself. "I am human. I feel pain, sadness, happiness…"

"That's not what I meant," Christopher said. "I know you have feelings. I only hope that this talk about the map hasn't caused you sadness as you thought about your father."

Raising her head, Belle took in a deep breath as she faced him. "My father didn't wish me to be a pirate."

"No?" Christopher could certainly understand her father's concern. He knew from his research that the life of a pirate was filled with danger. He imagined Belle had seen her fair share of it.

"He wanted me to be one of those boring women who sit at home doing needlework and playing the harpsichord."

"I can't imagine you doing either of those things," Christopher said.

"Nor could I. When I was old enough to do as I pleased, I used the education I received to my advantage. I did not wish to become some man's wife. I wanted something entirely different."

"What was that?" Christopher asked, although he was sure he already knew the answer.

Belle stood tall, throwing her shoulders back and holding her head high. "I wanted to captain my own ship."

Christopher couldn't contain the huge grin that appeared on his face. He had to admire her bravery. She didn't go into this life blind. Her father was a pirate, so she was aware of all the pitfalls and dangers involved. To pursue her dream, she had to be ten times braver than any man would have been. He was proud of her and imagined her father must have been as well. "What did you father think of that?"

"He was not happy at first, but I proved myself to him when I won *The Enchantress* playing Marias in a dockside tavern. The ship's captain was not happy with me. He threatened me with his flintlock pistol. His crew, who were not terribly fond of the man, had been watching as we played. They saw to it that I sailed away with my prize that night."

"I'm impressed." He meant it. Marias was a card game with a

thirty-two card deck, the suits of which were bells, hearts, leaves and acorns. He'd discovered in his research that it was a favorite among pirates. Winning something like a ship when gambling showed great skill on her part or her ability to cheat her way to a win. He preferred to think she won it fair and square.

"My father had no choice but to accept that his daughter was now following in his footsteps. I used the knowledge I had gleaned from my schooling and from my father to plunder many a ship, relieving them of all their treasure with nary a shot fired or a man killed."

"I'm doubly impressed. I don't understand why the English navy was after you then."

"I wasn't sure at first either, but then it came to my attention that a rival pirate, Blackjack Mills, sold me out to cover his own misdeeds." Belle took a deep breath. Her voice became harsh with anger as she spoke. "The man was a lying sack of eel guts. He knew that Captain Longworth of the British navy had been searching for the pirate who scuttled the English merchant ship carrying his fiancé. She'd been killed along with everyone on board. It was only a matter of time before the trail would lead to him and so I have it on good authority that Mills offered me up on a silver platter as the pirate responsible. If Longworth caught me there is no doubt I would be hanged." Her rigid stance fiery eyes were a marked contrast to the Belle she'd been only moments before.

"I'm so sorry that happened to you. What a terrible predicament he put you in." Christopher understood her anger. He was angry for her.

"Yes, but I am here now and safe from the captain." Her voice was harsh and low.

Christopher's eyes glanced off to the side as he thought. "Blackjack Mills. I've heard of him."

"And you've not heard of Silver Belle?" She seemed insulted. "How can that be?"

"I don't know. I've checked the history books since meeting you and it's almost as if you never existed."

The look on Belle's face was not one he enjoyed seeing. She was furious. Perhaps that bit of information should have been kept to himself.

"I hope you're not angry with me," Christopher said.

"It's not you that angers me." Her arms swept out, gesturing as she spoke. "You know my father, you know Blackjack and you know many others. Has history forgotten me because I was not a man? Or was it because I didn't leave a trail of bodies in my wake?"

He answered her honestly. It was what she deserved. "I don't know. I'll do more research and see if I can figure it out. I promise. And if I can't find anything, I'll personally make sure that you're not forgotten."

She visibly relaxed her shoulders. "You're a good man, Christopher."

"It's the least I can do for my treasure hunting partner." His smile was hopeful. He'd witnessed her sadness and anger at what had happened in her past. If he could fix it for her, he would. "Thank you for sharing your story with me. I feel that I know you a little better now."

Her face softened as did her voice. He could see that she was ready to put aside the sadness and anger for the moment and he wanted to help her do that with perhaps the only thing that might take her mind off of her past.

"Shall we continue searching?" he asked.

Without another word, Belle set her detector in motion and moved along beside the creek. Before long they were alerted to another metallic object buried beneath their feet.

Christopher dug in the spot Belle indicated and gasped as he pulled a silver drinking vessel from the sodden ground. "Belle, look at this!"

Holding her hand out she took it from him, examining it briefly before a wide grin appeared on her face. "Are there more?"

Checking the area, they found metal utensils and plates, but only the one silver cup. Further downstream they entered the creek and scanned along the banks that rose up out of the water. Before long there was another alert. This time they found a cloth bag filled with coins. Christopher handed it to Belle after examining them. "Those coins are from your time. Spanish pieces of eight. Not bad for a day's work," he said.

It was surprising the bag was still in one piece. Belle opened it and examined the contents. "How did they get here?"

"That's a very good question and one I don't have the answer to at the moment. It could be that the British soldiers that camped here had been carrying them. Perhaps they found them somewhere further south."

"I can't imagine I would ever leave a bag of coins like this behind." She placed the coins back in the bag and tried to hand them to Christopher.

"That's yours to keep," Christopher said.

"We should split it," Belle said, much to his surprise.

"I told you that anything you found was yours."

"I didn't find it. *We* found it."

Her generosity was unexpected. "Okay. I'll put it in my backpack and we can talk about it later when we get back."

A swift nod of her head and Belle was off down the creek. Christopher watched her as she swept the banks from top to bottom, while he continued searching in the area where the bag of coins had been found. It wasn't unlikely to find another in the same area. The metal detectors that he'd brought were fully immersible, so Christopher began scanning beneath the water of the creek. Much to his delight, he dug up two more bags of silver coins. He'd take a better look at them when they got back to the museum to see if there were any clues as to who may have left them there.

As was usually the case when Christopher was treasure hunting, the day passed by very quickly. They'd discovered more uniform buttons, utensils and more than their share of bottle caps and cans.

"We should get back to relieve Susanna," Christopher said.

"Thank you for bringing me with you," Belle said.

"I hope you enjoyed yourself." He knew to her it was work, but he thought she may have had some fun today. He certainly did. She had been good company and someone he wouldn't mind having with him on his next outing.

"I did. I would like to do it again…if you wouldn't mind bringing me with you."

He was surprised to hear a certain shyness in her voice that touched him. "I'd just been thinking that I'd like that very much. I believe there's more to find here."

They walked back to the car and as they came in sight of it, Christopher noticed a car pulling away. It kicked up so much dust that he couldn't see anything other than a dark vehicle speeding off.

"I wonder who that was?" he asked.

"Were we followed?" Belle asked. He could feel her natural wariness returning.

"I don't think so. It was probably someone stopping by to visit and when they saw that my friend wasn't home they left."

"Captain Longworth may have convinced Morwenna to bring him here so he could find me."

Wanting to put her at ease, Christopher asked, "Captain Longworth wouldn't know how to drive a car, would he?"

"No. He wouldn't," Belle replied, although the wariness he'd been sensing still remained. "Let's just check the house to make sure no one tried to break in." They put their things in the trunk of the car before going to the house and checking the doors and windows. "Nothing seems wrong. We should get going."

They got in the car and as Christopher backed out of the driveway, he hoped that his gut had been right on this one and that Belle's suspicions hadn't rubbed off on him. He shook off the uneasiness he was feeling and concentrated on the road and the woman beside him.

CHAPTER 9

The tavern was dimly lit, which only made the colorful Christmas lights strung across the bar and around the room that much brighter. Christmas music played in the background, while people smiled and laughed with each other, some exchanging early Christmas presents. Manning hated this time of year. The music, the lights, all of it brought back memories of that Christmas Eve when Maureen had kicked him out of *their* house and told him he should never come back. He scanned the room with disgust before taking a seat at the bar as he waited for Hunt to join him.

"How'd it go today?" Manning asked, when Hunt finally arrived.

"No 'hello, how are you'?" Hunt asked.

Manning shook his head, his thin lips forming a straight line that told Hunt exactly what he could do with his *hello*. "I'm not in the mood. All I want to know is how it went."

"Sure. Fine. I get it, it's Christmas." He patted Manning on the back. "I followed them from the museum. I'm pretty sure they didn't spot me." Hunt took the barstool next to Manning. "Whiskey on the rocks, please." he said to the bartender.

"Let's hope not," Manning said. Hunt didn't seem like the kind of guy who could easily hide himself, but people would be surprised. He was actually pretty good at hiding in plain sight.

The bartender placed a glass on the bar in front of Hunt before filling it.

"Put it on my tab," Manning said.

The bartender gave him the thumbs up before heading off to see to another patron.

"They went to someone's property out off Route 17 just north of the city. I don't know if they had permission to be there, but no one was home. They must know the people who live there because they didn't even check the house before wandering down to a creek on the property. I thought that was a little odd…"

"And…" Manning, interrupted him. He had little patience for Hunt's need to tell him every single detail about things that weren't of any significance.

"Nothing exciting. They spent the day looking for metal along the shore and in the creek." He took a large swig of whiskey and grabbed a napkin from a stack on the bar to wipe his lips.

"Did they find anything?" Manning asked. His patience was wearing thin. He wiped the condensation from his glass as he ran his fingers up and down the sides. He was nervous by nature and often found it hard to sit still for long.

"I wasn't close enough to get a good look, but they found a few bags. Mostly coins I think."

"Interesting. Do you think it was the treasure from the map?"

"Nah. This map seems to be for another spot." He pulled it from his pocket and examined it.

Manning shoved Hunt's hand as he quickly checked to see if anyone had been watching them. "Put that away."

Hunt shot Manning an irritated look before shoving it back into his pocket.

"I wonder why they didn't go looking for it." Manning rubbed his stubbled jaw as he thought about what that could mean.

"Who knows. Maybe she hasn't told him about it."

Manning continued stroking his chin before signaling the

bartender for a refill. "Well, keep an eye on them. If they find any real treasure we could both retire."

"Wouldn't that be nice," Hunt mused.

"Damn nice." Manning drained his glass. "Another please."

"You drink too much," Hunt said.

"That's not your business." Manning's tone remained cool though he knew Hunt was right. He did drink too much, but it helped calm his nerves.

"Maybe not, but I'm just watching out for you. I've known you a long time and I'd hate to see you in an early grave."

"I'm not going anywhere. At least not until we get our hands on that treasure. Then once we've got all the money we need, I can relax. I won't need to drink anymore." As much as Hunt drove him nuts sometimes, Manning appreciated his friendship. He'd been loyal and trustworthy since day one and so when Manning saw that map, he knew that the only person he'd be willing to share it with was Hunt.

Manning accepted another pour of whiskey, but Hunt covered his glass with his hand as the bartender attempted to pour him another. "No thanks."

A disapproving look came over Hunt's face as he eyed Manning's drink.

"Don't look at me like that. Geesh! You're worse than a nagging wife." A nagging wife he didn't have any more for that reason and a few others.

Manning couldn't stop thinking about the treasure map. "The treasure is important. We've got to be prepared to do whatever it takes to get our hands on it. Do you understand?"

"I get it," Hunt said. "You know, watching that chick, I might even believe she's a real-life pirate. That leather outfit she wears, which was minus the coins by the way, and just the way she handles herself. She had no problem shoveling through the muck in the creek. Pretty impressive. It's odd she's hanging out with the museum guy."

"Yeah. Especially since she broke in and tried to steal from his displays." It was a puzzle to Manning.

"Maybe he took one look at her and decided he'd rather get to know her better than press charges."

"She's an attractive woman," Manning agreed.

"I wouldn't mind getting to know her myself," Hunt said.

"She's way out of your league. So get that thought right out of your mind. Our main objective is to get the treasure. Don't forget it." Hunt had an eye for the ladies and could be easily distracted when he saw one he liked.

"I won't. I'll continue tailing them until we know where it is." Hunt pushed his glass away, leaned his elbows on the bar and folded his hands as though he was getting ready to pray.

"Good. Now if you're not going to drink anymore, you should go home." Manning knew he was being an ass, but that's what drinking did to him. Hunt only served to remind him of it.

CHAPTER 10

The small bistro just down the street from the museum was warm and welcoming as the group of four entered. Every table was filled with diners, as was the bar where bottles and glasses were displayed. They were seated by a fireplace near the center of the room and ordered their food from paper menus created especially for dinner that evening. Belle glanced around at the now familiar Christmas decorations, which she had to admit made the room especially festive. She couldn't help but be impressed with the food, the atmosphere and generally everything she was seeing in this lovely place. Dark wood paneling and low beamed ceilings reminded her of the captain's quarters aboard *The Enchantress*. She thought about her crew and wondered how they were getting along without her. She also thought about the ship's cat, One-Eyed Joe. Truth be told he was really Belle's cat. She had rescued him from a brawl with a larger orange tabby along the docks in Port Royal. He must be missing her terribly because she was certainly missing him and the way he snuggled up next to her in bed at night. Her one regret at this point was that she hadn't taken him with her and now with her future uncertain, she wasn't sure she would ever see him again.

"Are you alright?" Christopher asked. "You seem to have drifted away from us."

She answered, perhaps a little too gruffly. "I'm fine."

"That's good." Christopher was looking at her with some skepticism, as he turned to Edward and Susanna. "Are we all set?"

"Yes," Susanna said. Edward rose and gave her his hand, which she accepted. They then began to walk away.

Christopher was being very gentlemanly as he waited for her, but Belle didn't need his help.

"Go on. I'll catch up with you." She took one more moment to clear the memories from her head and then met the others at the door.

Now they were off to buy *Christmas* trees. And everyone seemed quite excited about it.

"I need one for the museum. Pirate themed I think," Christopher said. "And I should probably get one for my townhouse."

Belle simply did not understand what all the fuss was about, especially when she found out that Christopher intended to use his indoors.

"It's common practice in this time, you'll see. It will be beautiful," he assured her.

"So they are used indoors and outdoors as well? And not just in public places?"

Christopher turned in his seat to face her. "That's right. Some people even have artificial trees instead of the real ones. Personally, I prefer the scent of a fresh tree."

In order to prove the point, as they drove to the tree lot, all three of her companions pointed out every Christmas tree they passed. By the time they reached their destination, Belle was laughing at their antics.

Once they'd found the perfect trees, which seemed to take an unusually long time—they were just trees after all—they then looked to purchase all sorts of baubles for decorating. Belle had to admit that some of them were quite beautiful little treasures.

"Do you see any you like?" Christopher asked.

She held up a pretty red ball etched in gold. "This one."

"I like it. Put it in my basket and if you see anything else you like set it in as well." He went back to his search.

"You want me to help you?" Belle asked. She was both pleased and surprised. Was he just being kind?

Christopher put an odd-looking bauble he'd been examining back on the tree they stood in front of. He turned to look at her. His eyes were filled with sincerity. "If you wouldn't mind."

She didn't mind at all. "I would be happy to."

He smiled at her and she felt her tummy do a little flip. She hoped the oysters they'd eaten at dinner weren't spoiled. Following along behind him, she occasionally saw something pretty and handed it to him for approval before adding it to his other purchases. Glancing up at the top of the tree she saw a beautiful angel and whacked Christopher's arm to get his attention.

"Christopher. What about that one?" she asked, noticing his grimace and realizing that it probably wasn't a good idea to slap, punch, or kick someone to get them to look her way.

"I do need something for the top of the tree. I'll have someone get it down for us."

She didn't see who Christopher was speaking to because her attention was captured by the sweetest glass kitten. It reminded her of One-Eyed Joe. She held the glass kitten in her hand and hoped once again that he wasn't missing her too much. The gray tabby was her constant companion on the ship, following her everywhere she went. He was the one thing she'd allowed herself an attachment to. She gazed lovingly on the ornament before gently placing it in Christopher's basket. "And this one."

"Are you two almost done?" Edward asked from behind a cart filled to overflowing. "I'm glad we brought the truck. With any luck we'll fit everything in the bed."

"Let's hope," Susanna said.

"If not, we'll make two trips," Christopher added.

Belle helped load everything into the truck. Surprisingly it all fit, with the exception of a few things they held in their laps for the drive.

"We'll stop at the museum first," Susanna said.

"We can get the tree in some water now and decorate it tomorrow." Christopher glanced at Belle and with a tip of his head gave her a wink.

"Sounds good to me," Susanna said. "Next stop will be your place and then back to *The Dagger* for Christmas carols and hot chocolate."

Impressed as she was by their plan, Belle wished they could simply go back to the ship and sit around the fire as they'd done last night. She was feeling out-of-place with all of this Christmas excitement. Partaking in the celebration was usually left to others as Belle felt no particular connection to any of it. She'd celebrated as a child in London, but once she joined her father's crew on her twenty-first birthday, there had never been any time for it. His only interest was in finding as much gold and silver as he could while everyone else was occupied with their celebrations. She maintained that same philosophy when she had her own ship, although she did allow for the crew to do as they pleased if they were in port.

"Are you alright?" Christopher asked, seeming to sense that she had once again drifted off on him.

"I've never celebrated Christmas in this way. It seems strange to me."

"What about you, Edward?" Christopher asked.

"Christmas was special when I was a child and I brought that with me aboard *The Dagger*. We had no Christmas trees, but we drank and ate to our hearts' content. We sang Christmas carols and danced. Some of the crew would go home to their families or go ashore to celebrate with the locals in port. I quite enjoy the merriment."

Seeing the happiness and excitement shown by nearly every person they'd come across, as well as her three companions, Belle regretted that she hadn't taken the time to really celebrate Christmas. She was sure her crew would have enjoyed it, and now that she was experiencing it here in this time, she thought she would have as well.

They pulled up to the museum where they unloaded one tree and the bags of decorations that Christopher had selected for display in the main room. Next, they did the same at Christopher's home. The two-story brick townhome was connected to others in a row of five. They stopped right in front and carried everything up the stairs and through his front entryway. Belle was curious to look around, but there wasn't time as Susanna and Edward were in a hurry to get back to *The Dagger.*

"I'll give you a tour tomorrow when we decorate." Christopher seemed to intuitively understand what Belle was thinking as if by some magic. She was beginning to feel a connection to the man that was both unlikely and exciting.

* * *

THE DAGGER WAS COMPLETELY DECKED out in Christmas finery. The four of them had made quick work of it and were now standing back to admire what they'd accomplished.

"The trees look amazing," Christopher said. "I especially love the lights."

"You can never have too many," Susanna said.

Edward chuckled. "Not if you're Susanna Sutherland. Definitely not."

"You..." Susanna wrapped her arms around his waist and they shared a sweet kiss.

"I think this calls for a spiked hot chocolate," Christopher said. He gazed at Belle. A quick lift of his eyebrows invited her agreement.

"I would like that," she agreed.

"We'll leave these two love birds up here. You can join me in the galley and we'll whip something up."

He led the way down the stairs. Belle was right behind him. It made him happy that he seemed to be connecting with her. It had been a long time since he'd had a woman in his life. His wife Beth had left him when she realized he wasn't going to give up his treasure hunting for a *real job.* Now here he was sharing his knowledge with a woman who knew all about the excitement of uncovering treasure. Of course, Belle had her own ideas about where to get it, but she'd seemed very intrigued by what they'd done earlier in the day.

Christopher grabbed a pot from the rack above the stove, retrieved milk and a chocolate bar.

"Tell me how you make this. Is this the same chocolate as in the croissant I ate this morning?" She stood right beside him as he worked chopping the chocolate.

"Yes. Very similar." He broke off a piece, offering it to her. She opened her mouth and he carefully placed it on the tip of her tongue. "I'm going to melt the rest of it over a double-boiler." He showed her how he planned to do it and while the chocolate melted, he heated the milk. "Now, let me see…hmmm. Where is the coffee liqueur?"

Belle glanced around the galley. "Is this it?" She held up the bottle.

"That's the one. Can you stir the chocolate?" He handed her a wooden spatula and she went to work.

"Is it done?" Belle stood back so he could see what she'd done.

"Perfect. We're going to put it in with the milk and stir it around."

He poured the liqueur into each mug and topped it with the chocolate mixture. "Now for the fun part." Searching the refrigerator he found what he was looking for. He topped each mug with some whipped cream and shaved chocolate. Belle was fascinated with the container of whipped cream. "Here, hold out your finger." Christopher took the whipped cream from her and squirted some on her finger.

Belle stared at it and then at him.

"Taste it." He nodded towards her outstretched hand.

She stuck her finger in her mouth and when she removed it, a wide grin appeared.

"Well, what do you think?" he asked.

"More, please."

He lifted her chin in his hand and Belle didn't resist, which surprised him. He lingered there for a moment longer, gazing into her eyes and drinking in her beauty. He wanted to kiss her right then and there, but thought it might be too soon. Still, with her lips slightly parted…he stopped himself from following his instincts and instead said, "Open your mouth."

She did as instructed.

Christopher squirted whipped cream into her mouth and watched with amusement as she did her best to close her lips without losing any of it. A slight shriek and a giggle followed.

"I love showing you new things." He wiped her lips with a nearby kitchen towel, wishing that it were his lips instead kissing away any errant whipped cream. The thoughts running through his head were anything but chaste. It was torture thinking about those lips and so he forced his mind back to the task at hand. "We'd better get these upstairs before they cool off." *And hopefully so that I do too,* he thought.

From the look of her it was possible Belle was disappointed, but she was also good at hiding her feelings when she felt it necessary. He had a momentary regret at his lack of courage and wondered if he had kissed her would she have accepted it or would it have angered her. It was a question that was impossible to answer.

Once back up on deck, Belle stayed right by his side as they approached Edward and Susanna who were wrapped up in each other's arms and a blanket.

"Here you go." Christopher offered them each a mug.

"Thank you. Looks delicious," Susanna said.

"Mmmm…" Edward took a sip and his eyes lit up. "What's your secret?"

"I'm sure you can guess." Christopher waited for Belle to seat herself before handing her a mug and then took the spot next to her.

No one spoke as they enjoyed their hot chocolate. Christmas carols played over the speakers that were placed around the deck and before long, Susanna and Christopher were singing along while Edward and Belle looked on in amusement.

"All we need is some snow and it would be perfect," Susanna said.

"It's highly unlikely. Every now and again we get a tiny bit, but it's rare," Christopher said, gazing up at the sky.

"Too bad. I think it would be beautiful. We always had plenty of it in New York," Susanna raised her hands as if she could will the snow to appear.

"We can't have everything," Edward said. "But we do have each other, good friends and all of the other things that make for a wonderful Yuletide."

"I'd suggest a toast to all of us, but it seems we're out of hot chocolate," Christopher said.

"I can make some more," Susanna said.

"I should probably be on my way home. It's been a long day and tomorrow I've got a lot of decorating to do of my own." Christopher stood, smiling as he looked down at Belle and then to Edward and Susanna. He felt a certain contentment that had evaded him in the years since his divorce. Maybe the addition of two, time traveling pirates had changed his life for the better.

Edward collected the mugs and headed for the galley. "Good night."

Susanna followed along after him, leaving Christopher and Belle alone on deck.

Much to his surprise, Belle took his hand in hers. "I thought you were planning to kiss me earlier."

"I had thought about it," Christopher said. "I wasn't sure you would want that and I didn't want to assume you did."

"You are a gentleman." Belle moved closer.

"Is that a problem?" Christopher felt the warmth of her body and saw what seemed to be desire in her eyes.

"It doesn't have to be."

"May I…" The words were hardly out of his mouth when Belle's lips were on his, her body pressed close as her hands caressed his face. It was a blow-your-mind, sparks-flying type of kiss that he wished would go on forever. He barely had a chance to place his hands on her hips when it came to a stop. There was one more small peck on his lips as her hands slid down his cheek.

"Good night, Christopher." Belle turned and walked away leaving a very puzzled man in her wake.

"What just happened?" he muttered to himself. It took him a good minute to get his bearings before he was able to disembark and head back home.

CHAPTER 11

$\mathcal{B}$elle awoke thinking about the kiss. Despite living aboard a ship with a crew filled with men for most of her adult life, she had little experience with the tender side of men. Or at least, with men she liked and she liked this Christopher Plumb. She would also like to kiss him again and hoped she hadn't done anything to dissuade him. They barely knew each other, and yet she'd imposed herself on him in more than one way.

"Belle." Edward knocked on her door. "Susanna's going over to Christopher's. You can join her if you like, or you can stay here with me."

It wasn't a difficult choice. She definitely didn't wish to spend the day with Edward and she most certainly wanted to see Christopher again. It was a shame Susanna would be there as well. "I'll go with Susanna." She spoke through the door.

"I thought you would," Edwards voice teased. "Get dressed and meet her on deck."

Sleeping in hadn't been something she ever did, but thoughts of Christopher kept her enfolded in the comfort of her bed imagining that it was his arms she was wrapped in. Wanting to see him was just what she needed to get moving and before long she was up on deck and ready to go.

"How'd you sleep?" Susanna asked.

"Well, thank you."

"Christopher is waiting for us, so we should get going. I'm sure he will provide us with a breakfast of some kind since we're getting there this early, so we'll wait to eat."

Belle fell in stride with Susanna as they headed to the truck they'd ridden in the night before. It didn't take long at all to get to Christopher's house and Belle found that she had that same queasy feeling in her belly that she'd had last night. It hadn't been the oysters after all. It seemed her body had ideas of its own when it came to Christopher Plumb.

The front door of the townhouse opened as they got out of the truck.

"Good morning," Christopher stood waiting for them and looking even more handsome this morning than he had last night. His hair was combed neatly back, but one wayward lock fell across his forehead in a very enticing way. The silver strands in his hair gleamed in the sunlight, contrasting with the dark, almost black strands.

Belle almost tripped going up the stairs because she couldn't take her eyes off him. She was normally quite sure-footed, but something about this man was wreaking havoc on her normally controlled emotions. She was here to help decorate yet another tree and she was actually looking forward to it. She had disparaged ladies who needlepoint, thinking it a waste of time, but now she was rethinking her stance against all things ladylike. Since she'd been in this time, nothing she'd done had involved captaining a ship or piracy and yet she was enjoying herself very much. Life on land was different, but it could still be meaningful for her.

Christopher greeted Susanna with a kiss on the cheek and then he took Belle's hands in his. He gazed deep into her eyes. So deep in fact she thought he must be able to see the spot where her soul resides. Belle was very aware that Susanna was watching them with an amused expression and so she presented her cheek for him to kiss. He did so and without letting go of her hand, led her inside.

"You've got the tree up already," Susanna said.

"It's ready for decorations, as is the rest of the house." Christopher gently squeezed Belle's hand before letting go. "I did a little baking last night. It's probably not as good as Edward would do, but I think it came out pretty tasty."

"You made coffee cake." Susanna's excitement had Belle wondering what this coffee cake was.

"Let's hope that's what it turned into." Christopher laughed and his eyes crinkled at the corners. Belle didn't think she'd ever met anyone quite as happy as Christopher seemed to be.

"I'll be right back." Christopher headed for the kitchen.

"Is he always this happy?" Belle whispered to Susanna, feeling the suspicious side of her rearing its head.

"Pretty much." Susanna said. "But maybe a bit more than usual this morning."

"Let me help," Susanna said as he returned.

"I'll tell you what. If you get the coffee, I'll start unpacking the decorations."

"Deal," Susanna said. "I've got this under control, Belle. Why don't you help Christopher."

The tree was placed in front of a large window that overlooked the front yard. Although boxes were everywhere, Belle could see that Christopher's home was otherwise neat and clean. The furniture was sleek and unlike the ornate wood furniture of her time. Christopher was removing items from the boxes and setting them out in front of the tree.

As Belle moved closer to him, she breathed in the scent of him which was completely intoxicating. Closing her eyes she took in another deep breath and when she opened them, Christopher was smiling broadly in her direction.

Slightly embarrassed to be caught, Belle fessed up to the truth. "You smell..." She hesitated, not knowing how to describe the woodsy scent of him.

"Good, I hope." Christoper chuckled.

"Oh, yes, very good. It's just that I cannot place the scent."

"It's men's cologne. My favorite one in fact."

"I think it is now my favorite." Truth be told, it was much better than the smell of her crew when they'd been at sea for weeks. A simple bar of soap never seemed to be enough to wash away the smell of sweat, mingled with fish and salt water.

"I'm glad you like it."

The look he was giving her was melting her insides. She felt a bit like the giddy schoolgirls she remembered from her younger days at boarding school. They were always going on and on about some boy who'd caught their eye and then when they were older their interest changed to men of good standing who were wealthy and could provide them with all the beautiful things they wished for. Belle hadn't been anything like that. She didn't come from a home with a man of good standing in the community. John Silver was rarely around and Belle's mother, who was alone most of the time, wasn't much help when it came to helping Belle navigate the world of balls and upper-class nonsense. She was really never a part of it and everyone at school was aware that Belle came from a background very unlike any of theirs.

Christopher caught her eye again and Belle couldn't help herself. She moved closer, placing her nose as close to his neck as possible before backing away.

"Hey, you two. What's going on over there?" Susanna headed their way bearing a tray of mugs and cake.

"Belle was just telling me how much she likes the smell of my cologne."

Susanna inhaled deeply. "Mmmm…delicious. I love men's cologne. My favorite is the one Edward wears." She placed the tray on the low table by the settee. "Of course, I bought it for him."

Christopher handed Belle a plate with a piece of cake on it. "Try it. I'm curious to know what you think, and you don't have to spare my feelings. If it's terrible, let me know. I can take it."

Taking a small bite, Belle was pleased she didn't have to lie. "Delicious."

"I'm relieved. I was hoping to impress you with my baking skills, but they're really limited."

"Yummy," Susanna said before placing another forkful into her mouth.

Belle finished her cake as she examined some of the ornaments they'd pulled from the boxes. "Who is this?" She had never seen anyone in all her years at sea who looked anything like this man. He was portly, wearing a red suit with fur trim and a white beard. She had seen similar images of this man all over Charleston.

"That is Santa Claus. You might know him as St. Nicholas."

"He looks nothing like St. Nicholas," she scoffed.

"He's the modern day version."

Belle placed the ornament on the tree as they'd done last night on *The Dagger*. "Is this good?" she asked.

"Perfect," Christopher said. "Put them anywhere you like."

* * *

DECORATING the house for Christmas had been a lonely task over the past few years. Having Belle and Susanna here with him was making it so much more enjoyable.

"Look at this sweet little ornament," Susanna said, holding up a reindeer made of popsicle sticks and a red pompom nose.

"I made that when I was a kid. Second grade, I think," Christopher said, taking it from her and examining it.

"It's still in pretty good shape," Susanna said.

"I was an excellent craftsman back in the day."

"Did you make any others," Belle asked.

"I did, but I don't know if they've survived. My mother used to put them up on her tree, but she hardly decorates anymore."

"Where is your mother?" Belle asked.

"She's traveling right now. She lives here in Charleston, but both of my parents have always wanted to visit the Christmas markets in

Europe and so that's where they are right now. Maybe if you're still here when they get back, I can introduce you to them."

Christopher hoped she'd be staying around for a while, if not permanently. His feelings for her were developing more quickly than he would have thought possible and losing her wasn't something he wanted to think about.

"I would like to meet them," Belle said. "How do you think they'd feel about me being a pirate?"

"They'd love it," Christopher said, knowing they wouldn't be put off by it at all. They were incredibly open-minded and accepting people.

"I'm going to put on some Christmas music," Susanna said. "You two keep going. I know where everything is."

Christopher took the opportunity to pull Belle into his arms. "I'm so happy you're here."

"I am, too." Belle leaned in to kiss him, wrapping her arms around his neck and giving him a quick peck as Susanna returned.

Christmas music was now playing in the background, as Belle wandered over to look at the photos Christopher had displayed on a table behind the sofa.

"What are these?" she asked. "I've never seen anything like them."

"Those are photographs of my family." He held up one for her to see. "That's my mother and father in this one and those are my nephews and nieces."

"You are an uncle," Belle stated.

"My sister, Camille, and her husband have four children. They live in Ohio, so I don't get to see them very often."

"I like these photographs. They are not like portraits. They are real."

"A moment captured in time," Christopher said.

"I think this is it," Susanna said. "The last ornament." She placed it on the tree and they all stood back to admire their work."

"I can't thank you enough," Christopher said. "I dread doing this job by myself. It's always more fun with friends."

"You are very welcome," Susanna said.

"Look at the time." Christopher glanced at his watch. "I've got to get the museum open for the afternoon." He normally opened every day at noon and was open all day on the weekends when most people would be interested in visiting.

"We'll come with you." Susanna stopped abruptly, seeming to realize that she might not be needed any longer. "You know, I actually promised Edward I'd help him with some paperwork this afternoon. I'm so sorry. Maybe Belle can stay and help you."

* * *

THINGS COULDN'T BE WORKING out better for Christopher and at this rate he was sure this would be the best Christmas he'd had in ages. What more could he ask for? His two best friends and now a beautiful and intriguing woman who seemed as interested in him as he was in her. The only sticking point was that she was from another time and could possibly wish to return once she felt it was safe to do so.

They got the tree up and went through the boxes of decorations Christopher brought up from the museum basement.

"I'll bet you never imagined you'd be spending so much time helping me today."

"I've enjoyed it. It's not something I've done before."

"You weren't bored? I'm sure captaining a pirate ship is a lot more exciting."

"It can be, but there are long stretches out on the open sea when there is little to occupy the mind."

"Would staying here be hard for you? It would lack a lot of the adventure you've had in your life."

"It would be a different kind of adventure, I think," Belle replied. She gazed at the tree, lifting a small pirate ship in her hand that had been hung on one of the branches. "I have thought about what it might be like to stay here. There are many good reasons to stay. Not the least of which is safety, but I don't know how I'd feel about leaving my life as a pirate behind me forever."

He held a miniature Jolly Roger flag in his hand, twirling it back and forth as he spoke. "I understand. For selfish reasons, I wish you'd stay."

"You warm my heart and if I decided to stay, you would be the best reason of all." Belle went to him.

Christopher enveloped her in a hug. She rested her head on his chest. The feel of her there in his arms gave him some hope. In that moment he prayed that Christmas miracles really did occur. He sent his wish out into the universe knowing that Belle's decision would be one he would have to accept, no matter her choice.

After putting in a couple of hours, the museum looked like a winter wonderland with a pirate twist. He turned off his overhead lights and motioned for Belle to join him. Standing beside her he could feel a current bouncing back and forth between them.

"Are you ready?" he asked.

Belle turned to face him. "For what?"

"For this." With the flick of the light remote in his hand the tree and all the surrounding lights they'd installed that afternoon softly lit the museum, creating a warm and welcoming space.

Belle gasped and her hands flew to her lips. "It's so beautiful."

Christopher wrapped an arm around her shoulders and they stood together basking in the glow of the lights. This day had far exceeded his expectations. Belle was becoming so very important to him. The last thing he wanted to do was to think about what it would do to him if she left.

He could have stood with Belle in his arms forever, but she had other plans.

Reaching into her pocket she pulled out a paper he recognized as the map to her father's treasure.

"I have a proposition for you," she said. She carefully unfolded the paper and set it atop one of the glass cases.

Christopher moved to join her and stared down at what in this time should have been a worn and tattered paper, but instead looked almost new.

"If you help me find my father's treasure, I will split it with you,"

Belle said. An audible sigh escaped her lips as she looked down at the map.

His breath caught in his chest. This wasn't just a treasure, this was her inheritance. Her connection to her father. That she could even think about sharing it with him was overwhelming, not because of the money—he had more than enough treasure on display in the museum to live comfortably—but because she trusted him. Her trust was worth so much more than silver coins or sparkling jewels. "You don't have to do that Belle. I'd be happy to help you find the treasure. There's no need to share it with me. Your father wanted you to have it. It was his gift to you."

Glancing her way, he saw the narrowed eyes and frowning forehead of a woman who thought his answer strange. "You wouldn't make a very good pirate. None I know would ever pass up an offer like the one I've just made."

"I mean it. Believe me when I tell you I'm just happy to be of help."

Belle tapped on the glass of the case, staring down at the map and then quickly glancing at Christopher. "Alright. If that is your wish." She pushed the paper in his direction.

Christopher picked it up and examined it, the words Belle's Treasure were scrawled across the top. Searching for landmarks he might be familiar with but saw none. "Do you know where this is?"

"I'm afraid I don't," Belle said.

"Wait a minute I think I see something familiar, but it appears to be turned around." He went to his desk and retrieved a recent map of Charleston and the surrounding area. He laid it down beside Belle's map, studying them both. He stared at them for a good long while and then suddenly it became obvious to him. "It's upside down!"

Belle flipped the map so that Belle's Treasure was now at the bottom of the map. "Look, I thought these symbols were all chalices, but they were really bells all along."

"Very clever," Christopher said. "He used those bells to signify something."

"I think I see it." She lifted the map from the glass and held it up for Christopher to see. "My father disguised some of the features, but

I believe this is a river that leads from Charleston to the north. See, it's there on your map."

"Yes. I do see it. If I ignore the darker markings and focus on the lighter ones, I see the Cooper River. The bell symbols are dotted here and there alongside it. I've never hunted for treasure there so I'm not familiar with the topography of the area. It's pretty expansive, I'm not sure this is going to be as easy to find." As he stared at the map something jumped out at him. He hadn't seen it at first because it was cleverly hidden in an area that seemed to indicate brush or trees of some kind. He pointed to a symbol that looked different from the bells that were everywhere. It appeared to be a cross with a sword through it. What do you think this means?"

"That's my father's special mark. It should be where the treasure is located," she explained, peering closely at the spot he'd pinpointed.

"It's only about an hour and half drive from here. We could go tomorrow if you like." His eyes were bright with apparent excitement. "It won't be easy and we might not find it on the first try, but I'm eager to get started."

"Tomorrow it is."

"Do you think we'll need help?"

"The two of us should be fine."

"What if it's too heavy?"

She seemed to give that some thought. "If it is, then we'll bury it again and go back for it."

Christopher was impressed with Belle. She'd done this many times before and obviously knew what to expect. "We'll leave early in the day. It should give us plenty of time to locate the site."

"There should be a marker in the spot if I am correct."

"This is exciting. I'm looking forward to it."

"Are we done here?" Belle asked.

"I think so. Would you like to get some dinner?"

"Will we go back to *The Dagger*?" Her disappointment at that thought showed as she looked down at her feet.

Christopher took her hand in his. She gazed up at him with a resigned sigh.

"I've got somewhere special in mind. I think you'll like it," he said.

One of the colorful houses along Rainbow Row had been converted into a colonial style restaurant. He'd made the reservation earlier in the day, hoping that Belle would agree to dine with him. He was overjoyed that she had. Christopher led her to the door where he turned off the lights and after locking everything up took a moment to look into eyes that were now sapphire blue in the dim light of the street. He touched her cheek with his hand before brushing her hair back from her face.

"You do not need to ask me," Belle said.

Christopher took her in his arms as she tipped her head slightly to the side. His lips found hers and lingered there for first one kiss, then two. Before long it became apparent that passersby were watching them. Christopher took a step back. "We should go."

"Yes."

They strolled along wrapped in each other's arms. They went up Broad Street to Bay Street where the restaurant was located.

"This all looks familiar to me," Belle said.

"A lot of the buildings have been here a very long time, so I'm sure you've seen them before. The city has done an excellent job of preserving the impressive eighteenth-century architecture and colonial charm on Broad Street and many of the buildings are still used for their original purpose. Like those on the Four Corners of Law, which house a court house, the post office and city hall."

The restaurant's large porch was set up for dining with tables for two covered in white linens and wrought iron chairs with round padded cushions. Inside, the atmosphere was a bit more formal. More round tables set with fine china and silverware were festooned with Christmas decor and candles.

The hostess showed them to their seats and handed them menus. Belle seemed a little lost as she glanced from the menu to Christopher. "So many choices," she said.

"Would you like me to order for us?" he asked. "I know the chef here. I can have him put together something special just for us."

"That would be best," she said.

Christopher called the waiter over to their table and gave him instructions for the chef.

"Of course, sir. I'll take care of it right away."

In the blink of an eye, a bottle of champagne was opened at their table and two glasses were poured.

Christopher held his glass up and Belle did the same. "Here's to happenstance bringing us together."

They clinked glasses and drank.

"This is wonderful," Belle said before taking another sip.

"I thought you might like it." Christopher couldn't help but smile. He was enjoying himself immensely and it seemed Belle was too. Given the day they'd first met, he would have never expected to be lifting champagne glasses with her in a very romantic setting. For him Christmas had come early and given him a present he hadn't expected.

CHAPTER 12

That night in her bed, Belle thought she might be falling in love with Christopher. She'd never truly been in love before so the feeling was new to her. There certainly had been moments when she had been completely enamored with certain men in her past and as was always the case, they had disappointed her. Pirates didn't make for the best bedfellows and now that she'd met Christopher she understood why. He was nothing like them. Seemingly true to his word, he wasn't the type of man who would toy with her heart. She hoped he felt the same about her.

Sleeping seemed out of the question as she tossed and turned. They were going in search of her father's treasure the next morning and she wanted to be fully rested, but her body had other ideas. Throwing off the covers, Belle headed up on deck where she found Edward gazing out on all the boats in the harbor. Wrapped in her blanket, she joined him.

"Belle, this is a surprise," Edward said. He turned and leaned one elbow on the ship's rail as she joined him.

"I couldn't sleep."

"Too much excitement?" He wore a smug grin as he cocked an eyebrow. It was obvious he thought he knew something.

"Do not even begin to think of mocking me," Belle warned.

In typical Edward fashion he feigned innocence. "Belle, I would never."

"You would and you have," she reminded him.

"Alright, can you blame me for wanting to have a little fun?"

"Where is your wife?" Belle asked, glancing around the deck and not seeing her.

"Sleeping. Sometimes when it's quiet I enjoy standing here surveying my tiny domain."

She thought about her own domain. About *The Enchantress* and her life at sea. What would it be like to start over? Edward had done it, perhaps she could as well. "Do you miss it?"

"The sea?"

"Aye, the sea."

"Not as much as I thought I would. I tried staying in my own time but was alone and miserable. It occurred to me that I was afraid of what my life would be like without the excitement of being a pirate. It was foolish of me to think that way. I have everything I could ever want right here with Susanna. I am no good without her."

"You are a lucky man to have found her. Any woman who can put up with you deserves every honor."

"She does. I have become a better man because of her."

"Until now?" She'd noticed the change in him, but wanted to point out his mocking earlier.

"I'm sorry. It's been a while. Old habits die hard, you know." He grinned. "There's just something about you that brings it out in me." He tried to stifle his chuckle with a cough.

Belle furrowed her brow, giving him a sideways look. "Well stuff it back away wherever you've been hiding it."

"I will. I promise." His gaze left her and moved over the harbor. "How are you getting along with Christopher? Well, I assume since you spent the entire day with him."

"He is different." Her voice softened as she thought of him.

"In a good way?"

"Yes." Her answer came out on a sigh.

"Tell me about it." His voice lacked the teasing tone he usually took with her, letting Belle know he was truly interested.

"He asks permission to kiss me. At first I thought it odd, but now I think it is sweet. I like it. No one has ever asked me if they could kiss me before. They just did, whether I wanted it or not."

"Pirates…always taking what doesn't belong to them, even kisses."

Belle couldn't help but laugh. "I'll remind you that you were once one of them."

"You are right. I was. I've learned a lot from Susanna and from living in this time. I imagine you will as well."

"If I planned to stay, I imagine I would." Belle still couldn't commit to staying. There were many things to consider – her ship, her crew, whether she could settle in one place for any length of time. She thought about Christopher. He wasn't like the pirates she knew who were happy to come and go from ship to ship and port to port. He had roots here and he would stay.

"Be careful with Christopher's heart. Try not to break it. He is a good man."

"I am aware of the man that he is. I do not wish to harm him in any way." Belle gazed at Edward. It was good of him to care so much for Christopher. What he didn't know was that she did as well.

"Good. Because if you do, you'll have me to answer to and worse than that you'd have to answer to Susanna." He pointed a finger at her as he spoke. "They are the best of friends."

"Why did she not choose him over you?" Belle asked.

"Because I am irresistible." He tried to prove his point by cocking one eyebrow and curling his lips into a seductive grin.

Belle rolled her eyes and snickered. "You truly are full of yourself, Edward Sutherland."

"It's one trait I have yet to lose and I'm not sure I wish to."

"I'm not sure you can," she replied.

"The harbor is beautiful with all the lights reflecting off the water, don't you think?" Edward asked, changing the subject.

"I've never seen anything like it." It was true. She'd never seen so many lights in one place. They were magical.

"Wait until you see the parade of boats. You'll be amazed."

"I'm amazed by everything I see. The cars that move so quickly, the electricity that lights everything, the wonderful food. I could go on, but I'm sure the boats will be no different."

"They may be even more amazing than anything you've seen so far."

"We'll see." Belle said. She wanted to talk to Edward about the map, but she didn't want him tagging along with them tomorrow. In the end, wanting to know she was doing the right thing outweighed her caution. "Tomorrow Christopher and I are going in search of my father's treasure. I have the map he gave me and Christopher seems to think we can find the location, or at least come close."

"You have a treasure map?" It seemed Edward's interest had been piqued.

"I'm asking for your advice, not your participation," she said, wanting to make it clear.

"Oh." He sounded disappointed as his shoulders drooped forward and a pout appeared on his lips.

"Are you pouting?" Belle couldn't believe it. Edward was a grown man and here he was pouting like a small child.

"No. Of course not. I never pout. I was merely tugging at your heartstrings." He attempted to give her one of his most charming smiles.

"It won't work. Christopher and I are going alone."

"Then I wish you luck. Now what advice did you need?"

"I can trust him, can't I?" Belle asked.

"You were just telling me how different he is."

"He is different in a man and a woman way." She struggled to say what she was truly worried about. The men she knew from her time were much easier to read. She could tell immediately if they would be a good crewman, or if they were cheating at cards. She could even spot an English spy before even speaking with him. Christopher was so different from those men. She hadn't learned how to read him yet and it gave her pause. "I want to trust him with more than my heart."

"I believe you can. If there's one thing I know about Christopher, it's that he is a man of his word and a man who backs his words up with his actions."

"I offered him half the treasure and he said he didn't want any of it."

"I can see how that would raise your suspicions." Edward chuckled.

Belle was not amused.

"You asked for my advice. I think you couldn't be any safer than you will be with Christopher. He won't try to steal your treasure. He doesn't even want any of it. If you wanted to find someone to trust, then he's your man in more ways than one."

"I will take you at your word and I will trust him with the treasure. I believe he has already been entrusted with my heart."

Edward smiled from ear-to-ear. "Belle Silver you are in love."

His words took Belle by surprise. Could she really be in love? "I've never been in love, Edward. How do I know that's what I'm feeling and that it's not just desire?"

"I never thought I'd live to see the day when someone would ask *me* to define love." He placed a finger on his lips as he tipped his head up and looked off into the distance. "Well, do you think about him all the time? When you're together do you forget where you are and what you're doing? Do you feel like a new woman when you're with him?"

"Yes to all of those questions."

"Now, as to desire, it plays a large part in a loving relationship, so having desire for someone you love is a very good thing."

"I do desire him, but I don't know what to do."

"You don't have to do anything special. Continue to get to know him and more importantly put down the pirate guard you always have up and allow him to know you. I know over the years I've been hell-bent on giving you a hard time, but I've always known that you, Belle, were a damn good pirate. You are the very best life has to offer."

She was touched by his words. Coming from him it meant more than she could express. Instead of punching his arm, which would have been normal for her, she leaned in and kissed his cheek. "Thank you. I wish we had been better friends over the years."

"It wouldn't have been as much fun. Don't get me wrong. Just because I've become a more sensitive and caring man, it doesn't mean I wish I'd lived my life any differently. I believe it got me where I am today. So, don't disown your past. It's a large part of who you are but know that you can be so much more and do so much more when you have love in your life."

"If I hadn't heard it with my own ears, I would never have believed that such sage words came out of the mouth of Edward Sutherland."

He wrapped one arm around her shoulders. "I believe we need a drink to celebrate your newfound admiration of me."

She couldn't argue with him on that point. "Something warm to help me sleep. I've a big day tomorrow."

"A hot toddy should do the trick," he replied.

Belle walked along with Edward's arm still slung across her shoulders. She felt a closeness to him that had evaded her over the years. Not ever having a brother, Belle wasn't sure what that would have been like, but she liked to think of her new relationship with Edward as one of a brother and sister.

* * *

CHRISTOPHER GRABBED his backpack and tools from the closet at the museum. He told Belle he'd pick her up at *The Dagger*. The time they'd spent together the day before had awakened something in him. Something he hadn't felt in years and he was cautiously optimistic that this could turn into something special. There was always the possibility Belle would return to her own time, but he would do his best to convince her to stay.

Setting the alarm, he locked the door of the museum before heading for his car. A quick glance up and he briefly noticed a car parked across the street with a man inside who looked away when he met Christopher's gaze. He hoped the man hadn't been expecting the museum to be open today because if so he was out of luck. The museum had a steady flow of visitors, but his website recommended that people check in advance to see if it was open on any given day.

He knew that was disappointing to some, but he had to have time for treasure hunts and he couldn't do that if he was in the museum. Hiring someone was in his plans, but so far he hadn't found just the right person and so the museum remained closed on days when he was searching for treasure to add to the museum collection.

Belle was waiting for him as he pulled up. He got out and opened the door for her. She stopped before getting in and placed her hand softly on his before giving him a quick peck on the lips. Before she could pull away, he kissed her back with a long, slow, sensual kiss. He felt her collapse ever so slightly in his arms and his heart smiled because his lips were too busy to.

"Good morning," he said.

"Good morning," a very out of breath Belle uttered before hopping in the front seat.

Hurrying around to the driver's side, Christopher's pulse was still racing from the kiss they'd just shared. He was excited to search for the treasure, but he was more excited to be with Belle. She was the woman he'd always dreamed of being with—a treasure hunter like him, a pirate who had led a life that was of great interest to him and a woman who challenged him to step outside of his comfort zone and take chances. Belle was also curious, smart and had a good sense of humor.

Once he was on the main thoroughfare, he took her hand in his, enjoying the warmth of it and the willingness with which it had been given. The drive would be a little over an hour and then they would look at the map once again to see what their next steps would be.

"I'm excited about today," he said.

"Do you think we'll find it?" Belle asked.

"If we can find the landmarks on the map, we shouldn't have any trouble. Are you worried about that?"

"I wouldn't normally be, but this is my father's treasure. It's a treasure he wanted me to have. We are a few hundred years in the future and it's possible someone has found it by now."

"I think we've a good chance of finding it. I haven't seen anything about treasure being found near the area we're heading to. I keep a close watch on that kind of thing." He hoped that would put her mind at ease somewhat. "We'll stop when we get closer to make sure we know where we're headed. We may have to hike in with our equipment. Let's hope it's not too far."

"I hadn't thought of that." A soft smile appeared as she looked his way.

Some of the pirate that he'd seen in her on day one had disappeared and seated beside him was a woman he could see himself loving for a long time.

"How long do you think you'll stay in this time?" He tried to sound as casual as possible and not like a man who desperately hoped she'd say forever. If she had plans to leave it would hurt, but it was better to know.

"My initial plan was to stay until I felt it was safe to return. At this point, I'm not sure if that will ever happen. I do know that I miss my crew. I miss my ship and I miss being in control of my own life."

"I know it's a difficult choice, but if it were up to me I'd want you to stay. Old Christopher would have told you it was okay if you decided to go back. This Christopher wants you to know that if you stayed it would mean the world to him."

"I still need time to think. It is a big decision, but if I do stay it will be because of you."

Christopher wanted more than anything to take her in his arms at that very moment. If only he wasn't driving.

They reached the turn off he'd been looking for and he pulled off to the side of the road. Belle handed him the map and he followed the route faintly outlined on the map with his finger, comparing against the roadmap he brought. One thing he'd always been very good at was deciphering old maps. He'd done it many times over the years and with much success. "I think I know where we need to go and it's not by the water. We'll have to hike in from a town on the outskirts of the lake area. Hopefully we can get as close as possible."

CHAPTER 13

*L*uckily for Hunt and Manning, Plumb hadn't noticed they had been following him and were now parked a few hundred yards away in a shaded spot that afforded them some much needed cover.

"This is it," Manning said. Adrenaline was coursing through his veins as it always did when he was about to win big in an investigation.

"Are you sure?" Hunt asked, seeming out of sorts.

"Why else would they be coming all the way out here?" Hunt's attitude was typical for the guy. It irritated Manning, but he was the boss on this one and Hunt had little say in anything they would be doing today.

"I don't know…maybe to do some metal detecting like they did the other day. This could end up being a complete waste of our time." Hunts lips pressed together in a thin line. Doubt should have been his middle name. It was amazing to Manning that he was such a good private detective and it frustrated him that on this day, when they could score big, those doubts were obviously erupting in Hunt like lava flowing from a volcano.

"If we don't follow them, how else are we supposed to know when they find the treasure?" Manning was irritated that Hunt was eating into his excitement and it showed. He drew in a long breath to calm himself before he said something he'd regret. "I have a good feeling about it." He paused to taking a sideways glance at Hunt. "Hopefully I'm right."

They waited patiently for the car to get back on the road and when it did they followed along at a distance that might just keep them from being noticed. They were headed for a small town just north of the exit. One Manning was familiar with. The town of Ammea Creek was home to slightly more than a few dozen people. Manning had once gone to school in the next town over and had a high school sweetheart who lived in Ammea Creek. It was another relationship that had not ended well for him and one he would prefer to forget about it. The town's main street was nothing more than a two-pump gas station attached to a small grocery store. Not a soul seemed to be around, which would work well for the two detectives once they had what they came for.

"So what's the plan?" Hunt asked once they had reached the town.

Manning had his eye on Belle Silver and Plumb. "I like to fly by the seat of my pants most times, but here I think we just watch and wait. Who knows if this is even the right location?"

"We better hope it's in a wooded area, otherwise they'll spot us for sure." Again, Hunt's negative Nelly attitude was coming out.

Manning squashed that doubt right away. "From the looks of those two, they seem so interested in each other that we may not have to worry about being seen. At any rate, we'll play it by ear. I've got some ideas, but nothing set in stone."

"Like what?" Hunt asked.

"Nothing you need to know about right now." Manning didn't want Hunt fretting about something that may or may not happen. "I'll fill you in when the time is right. For now, we'll follow along behind them at a safe distance. Hopefully they stay on the hiking trail, which will make it easier for you and me."

"I'm not in the greatest shape." Hunt seemed worried from the sounds of it.

"I'm aware," Manning said, eyeing Hunt's slightly protruding belly.

Hunt sucked his belly in and straightened his shirt. "Hey, give me a break. I spend most of my days in my car watching and waiting. I don't usually have to go hiking on the jobs I take."

"Sorry. I shouldn't talk. Being a detective leaves little time to spend at the gym."

"Okay, so we'll hope neither one of us has a heart attack because it looks like we'll be heading uphill." Hunt pointed to Belle and Plumb as they started hiking.

"Hey, I'm not that out of shape," Manning protested.

"And neither am I." Hunt was still holding in his gut, which caused Manning to chuckle.

"I have a better idea. Instead of killing ourselves with this hike. Let's wait here for them. They have to come back for the car, right?"

"I see what you mean and I agree wholeheartedly." Hunt appeared happier on hearing this plan.

Manning parked the car behind some trees that would make it hard to see and they settled in to wait.

CHAPTER 14

"This is as close as we can get," Christopher said.

It was still morning, so they had plenty of time to locate the treasure. He had parked the car with convenience in mind, off the road behind some trees where they were almost completely out of sight. If they found something, he wanted to be sure they could load it into the car without being observed. The walk from this point shouldn't take long if he'd calculated their location successfully.

Belle got the backpack Christopher had packed for her and slung it over her shoulder before grabbing the equipment. Each would carry a metal detector, shovels, pinpoint locators and large scoops to sift through the dirt they would be digging up.

"Ready?" Christopher asked.

Belle nodded and began walking along beside him. They went as far as they could before the path narrowed and forced them to walk single file as they headed up a steep incline. Christopher took the lead.

A branch cracked behind them.

"What was that?" Belle asked, turning to look.

"Nothing to worry about. Keep your eye out for wildlife, we're in their world now."

It was no secret that the waterways had a fair share of alligators and poisonous snakes. They were far enough away that they didn't have much to worry about from them, but bears could be a concern.

Belle wasn't so sure it was a bear and she definitely didn't think it was nothing. She kept herself alert and her flintlock at the ready for any further indication that someone or something might be following them.

Christopher stopped and took out the map. "We should be getting close." He pointed to a symbol on the map. "What do you think that means?"

It was a triangular shape that surrounded a circular maze-like pattern. The symbol was one that her father used often to indicate something of value, especially when blazing a trail that he expected to return to in the future. "We should keep our eyes open. It is most likely inscribed on a rock somewhere up ahead."

They reached a switchback path with a high rock wall to one side. Belle stopped to examine it. "There," she said. Not far above eye level there was a carving in the rock wall.

"Is that it?" Christopher asked,

"I believe so." Belle squinted her eyes against the glare of sunlight making it difficult to see. She shaded her eyes with her hands and took a closer look. "Yes, that's it!" It was her father's signature symbol, the cross and the sword. John Silver had been here and left his mark for Belle to find. "Thank you," she whispered, hoping that somewhere out there in the vast unknown, her father might hear her.

"Do you think the treasure is buried around here?"

Belle looked around. It didn't seem likely from the looks of their surroundings. "I think it's letting us know we're on the right path. Look at the map. Are there more symbols?"

Christopher held the map out so they both could see it and placed his finger on the symbol they had just found. "This is the spot."

"No. There's one more," Belle said, pointing to a barely visible spot on the map. "Up ahead."

They trekked up the steep incline and when they reached the top it opened out into a flatter wooded area. Belle took the lead and walked out to a spot that held a familiar clue. There in the midst of all those trees was a good-sized boulder and on it was another of her father's symbols. The one he used to indicate buried treasure. She turned back to Christopher. "This is it!"

He hurried to her side and surveyed the area. "Is it under the rock?"

"Possibly. We'll have to move it to find out." Belle walked around the boulder and didn't see anything that would indicate otherwise.

"First let's try the detector." Christopher turned it on and moved around the rock. As he got closer, it sounded an alarm. "You're right. we'll have to move it."

"Maybe if we dig around the bottom on one side we can push it out of the way."

"It looks to be quite heavy. It could be around half a ton easily." Christopher said, as he glanced around at the bottom of the rock. "Lucky for us, I think I brought the exact equipment we're going to need." Slipping his backpack from his shoulders he unzipped it and took out a length of heavy strap and a tool called a come-along.

"What do you intend to do with those?" Belle asked. "I brought a hand spike, wouldn't that do the same?"

"It would take a lot longer and a lot more muscle. I don't know about you, but I prefer to take the path of least resistance." Christopher wrapped the strap around the middle of the boulder and the trunk of a large tree then winked at Belle. "With any luck we'll have this boulder moved in no time."

Belle was skeptical that it would work, but she'd seen so many useful tools in this time that she would wait and see if it worked before offering the hand spike. She watched as Christopher cranked the handle of the come along, which then tightened the strap and eventually began moving the boulder towards Christopher.

"Do you want to do this, and I'll give the boulder a shove to help move it further?"

"You keep doing that. I'll push the boulder." Belle was perfectly capable of moving the rock. She wasn't a dainty little woman who needed help from a man, even if it was Christopher. She was a pirate captain after all.

A few more cranks of the handle and a shove from Belle and the boulder was now out of the way.

"We make a good team," Christopher said.

"I have been thinking the same," Belle said, flashing him a brilliant smile.

"We'll rest for a minute and then start digging."

Belle sat, resting her head on the boulder behind her. When her father had given her the map she never expected it would be this easy to find. If it wasn't for Christopher, it might not have been. She reached out and took his hand in hers. "Thank you."

"For what?" he asked, joining her, and leaning his shoulder on hers.

"For helping me find the treasure." She enjoyed the feel of him right next to her and she would have sat like that for hours if it wasn't for the treasure calling to her. Belle was excited to find out exactly what John Silver had left for her. Silently thanking her father once again she was sure that he would have been astounded that she'd not only traveled through time, but by car to reach this spot. It would have been a much harder trek for him, taking days or even weeks.

Christopher was watching her with those sweet, soft eyes of his. This man had sacrificed time and energy to help her. "We haven't found it yet. We've got work to do if we're going to locate it before the sun goes down."

"I'm not leaving until we do," Belle was determined to dig this treasure up here and now.

"We'll stay here tonight if need be."

Belle considered herself incredibly lucky to have him with her, willing to stay no matter how long it took.

Christopher stood and held out a hand to Belle. She didn't need it to rise, but she took it anyway. He was her partner in this venture and she was grateful to him for the many things he'd taught her since she arrived.

They began digging and about two feet down they hit something hard.

Belle brushed the dirt off around it and saw a slightly rounded item that could be the top of a chest. "This is it," she said.

* * *

CHRISTOPHER LOOSENED the dirt around the edges, being careful not to damage the chest. He was first and foremost an archaeologist even if he'd never fully pursued that career. After an hour of careful digging, he felt it would be safe to attempt removing the chest.

"I'll get this side and you take that one," he said.

Belle followed his lead, reaching down beside the now exposed chest. It was a dark brown, no doubt from being buried in dirt for all this time, but it was in surprisingly good shape.

Lifting it out, they set it on the ground between them.

"This is it, Belle. You must be elated," Christopher said.

"More than you know," Belle stood staring at the chest with what seemed a mix of sadness and triumph.

"Are you going to open it?" Christopher asked.

"Yes, of course." Belle dropped to her knees and Christopher joined her. "It's locked."

"Hmmm… We could smash it, but the archeologist in me feels funny about doing that."

"I've got something." She reached into a pouch she wore strapped across her body and removed what Christopher recognized as a lock pick.

"Perfect," he said.

Belle went to work and in short order had the lock opened. She lifted the top of the chest, gazing into it with a wide-eyed expression.

Christopher equated it to a kid on Christmas morning. He couldn't imagine what she must be feeling at this moment.

The chest was filled with everything from gems, to eighteenth century jewelry. They could see gold coins nestled in between chalices and a pocket watch that caught Christopher's eye. He lifted it from the chest and held it in his hand, aware of the fact that John Silver had once used this watch. An envelope peeked out from the treasures they were examining.

"It has your name on it," Christopher said.

Belle opened it and unfolded a letter addressed to her from her father.

My darling daughter,

If you have found this letter, I congratulate you. You were always my special girl and I could think of no finer way to provide for your future than with the contents of this box. I never wished for you to be a pirate, you know that. But I was proud of all your accomplishments at sea. This chest is for you. If you find it and wish to retire, I will be happy, but if not I understand. It will be for your future. Use it wisely and please, if you wish to continue pirating, be careful. There are vultures around every corner.

With much love,

Your Papa

Belle sat staring down at the letter before holding it close to her heart.

Christopher handed her a hanky from his pocket and understanding that she didn't wish him to see her cry, he walked away for a moment, giving her time to grieve the loss of her father and to absorb the words of his letter.

When she was ready, they closed the chest and each took a handle as they headed down the hill, clutching the rest of the gear in their free hands. Belle was quiet as they walked. Christopher understood why. This treasure was of great importance to her and her search for it was now over. He wondered if the words her father had written would give her reason enough to retire from piracy. Knowing Belle, he knew that would be a difficult decision for her.

After having to stop many times to rest, they reached the bottom of the trail, relieved to finally roll the strain out of their shoulders and wiggle their fingers.

"There's the car," Christopher said and as he did, he noticed a second vehicle parked nearby. They hadn't met anyone on the trail, but there didn't seem to be anyone around either.

They placed the trunk down behind the car while Christopher searched for his keys in the backpack.

A noise behind them caused them both to spin around. Two men stood facing them, guns aimed in their direction.

"Where did they come from?" Christopher asked.

"They must have followed us," Belle said.

"It's about time," the taller man said. "We've been waiting for you for quite some time."

The two men moved toward them. Christopher's heart was beating rapidly in his chest, but when he glanced at Belle, he could see she was as cool as could be. This was the pirate queen Silver Belle. Her cold and steely gaze should have told these men they were in trouble, but their guns were giving them a false sense of security. If he was a betting man, he'd be betting on Belle to come out the winner.

"If you don't mind, we'll take that with us," one of them said.

"I do mind," Belle said, taking a step towards them.

"I wouldn't do that if I were you," the taller of the two men said, raising the gun towards her.

Christopher panicked. She could be shot dead at any moment and he couldn't lose her, not now. "Belle, let them have it. It's not worth losing your life over."

"I don't intend to lose my life." She eyed the tall man. "I saw you at the police station. You took my things away."

"I did. I copied your map thinking I'd search for it on my own, but following you was easier." He chuckled, which Christopher under-stood to mean this guy was in charge and he wasn't planning on giving up the chest.

"You were parked outside of my museum the other day," Christo-pher said to the other man.

"What if I was?" the man asked in a surly tone.

"You won't get far with it. We have friends who know where we are," Christopher said.

"That's a shame. If you hadn't recognized us things might have turned out better for you." He aimed the gun at Christopher, seeming ready to pull the trigger.

"I don't think we want to leave any evidence behind. As far as anyone knows they came out here and got lost," Hunt said.

Manning thought about that for a moment before agreeing with him. "You two put the chest in the trunk of my car." He waved the gun in the direction he wanted them to go.

Belle eyed Christopher in a way that said she wasn't planning to go quietly. He leaned in and whispered to her. "Let's do what they want until we see how this is going to play out."

She closed her eyes and blew her breath out through her nose.

Two guys with guns were nothing to fool around with. They had to wait for their opportunity and even then, things weren't looking good.

"Let's go," Hunt said. He waved his gun at Christopher, indicating the chest.

Christopher and Belle each took a handle and walked to the now open trunk, placing it inside.

"What's inside?" Manning asked once he'd closed and locked the trunk.

"My inheritance," Belle snarled.

"That's got to be worth some nice ka-ching," Hunt said with a laugh.

"Where to?" Hunt asked.

"I've got my boat docked nearby."

"You've still got that thing? I thought your wife got everything."

"She did, but I got this one from someone who owed me a favor. I still like to fish some weekends and leaving it up here is cheaper than in Charleston Harbor." He motioned for Belle and Christopher to move to the side of the car. "We'll take these two with us. We can dump them once we're far enough offshore and then head for Florida. I've got a friend there who can help us with the treasure."

"You're not going to get away with this, you spineless bilge rats!" Belle was seething. Christopher could feel the anger spilling off of her in waves.

"That's a good one," Hunt laughed.

"You'll see just how good it is when I get my hands on you," she shouted.

"Belle, don't waste your energy," Christopher whispered.

Belle, now looking daggers at him, didn't listen. Why would she?

She'd probably never met someone who would have allowed this to happen. She lunged at Hunt who was the one nearest to her and as she did Manning's gun came down on her head. She dropped to the ground and didn't move.

"Belle!" Christopher shouted. He tried to go to her, but Manning shoved the barrel of his gun in his back.

"Shut up and put your hands on your head." Manning tossed a set of handcuffs to the other man, "Cuff her," he said as he took out a second pair. His arms were bent awkwardly behind his back as Manning pushed him into the back seat. They gathered up the unconscious Belle and shoved her in beside him.

Her body slouched against his, her head on his shoulder. He kissed the top of her head and silently promised he would do everything in his power to make sure she got out of this.

* * *

By the time they got to the marina, it was dark. Manning hurried Christopher onto a twenty-five foot cabin cruiser while Hunt slung Belle over his shoulder, grunting and groaning all the while. He double checked the cuffs to make sure they were secure and then locked them below deck along with the treasure chest.

The sound of the boat alerted Christopher that they'd be moving soon. Beside him, Belle stirred. With his arms shackled behind his back, he was frustrated that he couldn't do anything to help her.

"Belle, are you okay?" he asked, hoping she could hear him.

She struggled to sit up, the cuffs on her wrists making it obviously more difficult. "Where are we?"

"We're on a boat heading out to sea."

She nodded and he could see her formulating a plan in her head.

"I'm sorry I couldn't do more to stop them. I'm sure you're disappointed in me."

"You did what you thought best. There's still time to stop them."

"How? Our hands are cuffed behind our backs." He had faith in

Belle, but from his standpoint it looked like a pretty hopeless situation.

Belle scooted closer to him, positioning her back to him. "Can you reach the pocket of my jacket?"

"I think so. What am I looking for?" He moved as close as he could.

"My lockpick set. I put it in my pocket instead of in my pouch."

"That's lucky," Christopher said as he tried to fish his hand inside her pocket. His movements were awkward and the numbness of his fingers wasn't helping, but eventually he found the lockpick and managed to get it in his hand.

"Give it to me," Belle ordered. "I'll unlock you first and then you can get mine." She silently went to work and before long the cuffs came loose. Christopher shook the blood back into his hands. "Here."

He took the lockpick from her hand, examining it. "I've tackled rusty old locks before, but never police-issued handcuffs. I wonder if they work the same." He took the slender metal tool and by some stroke of luck was able to unlock her cuffs without much trouble. He was pretty pleased with himself.

Belle held a finger to her lips. Neither one of them spoke as they waited and listened. Activity on deck came to a halt as the boat slowed.

"They've entered the harbor," Belle said. "It won't be long until they are out on the open sea."

"What's our next move?" Christopher asked, more than happy to leave the rest of their escape up to her.

"They took my flintlock pistol, but they didn't get all of my weapons," Belle said. She had a devious smirk on her face as she tipped her head towards her boots.

"Are you sure? It looked like he nabbed more than just the flintlock before getting you in the car."

"I'm very sure."

"Have you got something there?" he asked, pointing to her boots.

"I have many somethings," Belle replied with a grin.

"Now what?" Christopher wondered out loud.

"Here," Belle handed him a pistol she extracted from the lining of her jacket. "You get one shot, don't waste it."

"I can't believe he didn't find that one." He held the antique gun in his hands, appreciating the beauty of it and the way it fit perfectly in his palm. "This is beautiful," he said.

With a pistol in one hand and a dagger in the other, Belle's eyebrows shot up as she gave him an exasperated look. "You can admire it later. They will want to get away from the city so as not to be seen, we'll wait for them to come to us."

"We aren't going to kill them, are we?" Christopher had never thought he'd find himself in a situation like this. The thought of killing someone didn't sit well with him.

Belle looked him in the eye, her voice very low and serious. "Never hesitate. Our lives depend on it. Remember they are planning on killing *us*."

A nervous laugh escaped his lips. While he had been thankful to see her pirate guard fall as she began to trust him, he was quite happy to see it back in place. This was the pirate he first met a few days ago. She knew all too well that relying on him to rescue them was a fool's dream. He was a man of knowledge and not a man of battle. If they were going to get out of this, it would be because of Belle.

* * *

BELLE WAS in her element here and she could see that Christopher wasn't. She put down the dagger and reached for his arm with a reassuring smile. "This is going to end either one of two ways. With them bound and gagged, or dead. Christopher, I know this is not something you've ever had to do before, but I have…many times. Now, point the gun down at your side and take a deep breath to stop shaking."

Christopher did as she asked, the tension in his body relaxing with each exhale. "I'm fine," he said. "Just nervous energy."

"My guess is one of them will stay topside while the other is down here. Separated they will make easier targets. Do you trust me?"

"How could I not trust Silver Belle, notorious pirate queen of The Golden Age?"

Belle stifled a laugh as she retrieved her dagger and they waited, listening to footsteps above and the sound of the engine whirring as they cruised full speed through the waters off the coast.

They didn't have to wait long before the engine quieted. Christopher glanced Belle's way and she silently nodded to him before stationing herself in such a way that when the door opened, she would be hidden from view. "Stay where you are and point the gun at the door."

On *The Enchantress*, every man was skilled with swords and guns, it was a requirement on a pirate ship. But Christopher wasn't a pirate. He was a man she cared about and wanted to protect at all costs. Deep down she realized that she would even leave her father's treasure behind if it meant that Christopher would be safe. Footsteps heading down the stairs stopped outside the door. Christopher's mouth went dry as his heart raced in his chest. Belle on the other hand seemed coolly without emotion.

As the door opened, Hunt stopped short. He carried no gun, which came as a surprise.

"Come in," Christopher said with a surprisingly steady voice. Belle couldn't help but smile a little at that.

As Hunt did as he was instructed, Belle grabbed him from behind, wrapping an arm around his neck and placing her gun at his back.

"How did you…?" He stuttered and stopped.

"Never mind that," Belle said.

They tied him up, binding his hands and feet together with a rope they found stashed in a corner. They were sure to tie him in such a way that he wouldn't be able to get himself out of the bindings.

"Hunt? Where are you? Bring them up." Manning called from above.

Hunt looked like he was about to call out, but Belle reminded him she had a gun pointed at him.

"He's waiting for me up there," Hunt said.

Belle started up the stairs to the deck with Christopher following behind her. She had noticed many of the boats tied up near *The Dagger* had few places to hide on deck. Once they were clear of the hatch, they would be easy targets.

As they reached the top step, Belle stepped out on the deck first followed by Christopher, cautiously glancing around. "Where is he?" he whispered.

Belle motioned for him to stay put while she circled the deck of the boat.

A blinding flash and a loud crack came from behind, then Christopher fell to the deck.

CHAPTER 15

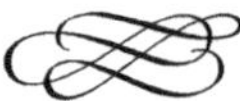

*B*elle ducked behind the bulkhead and watched Christopher's chest rise and fall with steady breaths. He was alive, for now. There was no choice but to prepare for battle with Manning who was somewhere nearby and waiting for her. If she failed, they would both find themselves floating in the Atlantic Ocean and these men would get away with her father's treasure.

Seeing Christopher laying limp and unconscious angered her. He didn't deserve this. All he'd done was help her find her father's treasure. Her blood was boiling, but she did as she always did when faced with a situation like this. Remaining calm and thinking clearly were important if she was going to succeed. Manning had no idea what he was about to face, but Belle knew there was no choice other than to take him down.

"I know you're there," Manning said. "Come out where I can see you so we can talk about this."

Belle didn't move. She wasn't in a good enough position to avoid getting shot. He had to be in sight if this were to work. She waited patiently hoping he wouldn't harm Christopher any further.

"Where's Hunt?" Manning asked.

"Down below. He'll be no help to you," Belle answered.

Belle could hear him moving but couldn't see him. Her keen hearing told her he was up above her. If she came out onto the deck he was in a perfect position to take her down. That wasn't going to happen. He obviously didn't know Silver Belle. If he did, he might be shaking in his boots. Crouching low, she listened for any further clues as to his location. He was breathing heavily, obviously nervous about what would happen next. That was a good thing. She stood a better chance if he was fretting.

Christopher groaned and moved. He was coming to. Belle hoped Manning hadn't noticed, but it seemed he did. He went to Christopher and pushing the gun out of reach, sat him up. "I've got your man," Manning said. "Come out now or I'll be sure to finish what I started."

Belle stayed where she was.

"Throw whatever weapons you have out on the deck and I'll let him live."

She knew that wasn't the truth. He planned to get rid of them as soon as he had the advantage. Why would he wait? Still, she had to do something. Never one to back down from a fight, she emerged from the bulkhead.

"I said toss your weapons." Manning pointed his gun in her direction.

Belle gazed at Christopher. His shoulder was bleeding, but he seemed okay. She tossed her gun and dagger onto the deck.

"Where's the rest of it?" he asked. "I filled a whole box at the station the day you were arrested. That's the last time I let Hunt search anyone."

"It's all I have," she lied.

"I don't believe you."

"See for yourself," she said.

Manning stood, leaving Christopher where he was. It was obvious he didn't see him as a threat in the condition he was in.

Belle stood her ground as Manning approached and silently sent Christopher a message with her eyes. *It's going to be alright.*

It was a tricky maneuver for Manning to frisk her and also keep the gun pointed at her.

"Put your hands on your head," he said.

She did as she was told and as he leaned down to check for weapons in her boots, she slipped a dirk from her sleeve and brought the pommel down on his head. Manning crumpled to the deck but she could tell from the curses he was shouting that he was still conscious. He aimed his gun ready to shoot, but Belle kicked it out from his hand. He started to crawl after it and she took advantage of his prone position. Putting her knee on his back, she grabbed his arm and twisted it behind him. She felt his shoulder dislocate and heard the guttural scream emanating from him as he squirmed in pain.

"Christopher, can you get me some rope?" Belle asked.

Getting to his feet, Christopher's surprise was evident in his dazed expression and shaky voice. "Are you okay?" he asked. His hand went to his shoulder.

"I'm fine. We're going to be fine. Now get the rope and help me tie this bilge rat." Belle made sure to grind her knee further into Manning's back and had no pity for him when she saw tears sprout from his eyes.

"Here's the rope," Christopher said.

"How's your shoulder?" Belle asked.

"Painful, but I'll be alright. I'm lucky it was just a flesh wound. Apparently our Mr. Manning isn't a very good shot, but I must have hit my head on something when I fell."

They tied Manning as they'd tied Hunt. Belle had no mercy for the man or his dislocated shoulder. "If you don't stop squirming I'll toss you overboard," Belle growled in his ear.

"Do you know how to get us back to shore?" Christopher asked. "I'm a little turned around out here."

"I'll get us back to Charleston if you show me how to operate the boat."

"I can definitely do that," Christopher said.

Belle made sure that Manning and Hunt were both secure and would be no further threat to them and then went to stand by

Christopher as he gave her a quick lesson in operating a modern-day boat. Belle turned the boat around and set them on a course for home.

"You were amazing," Christopher said.

"I wasn't about to let that man hurt you again," Belle said.

Christopher reached for her with his uninjured arm and pulled her close. "Thanks for saving me."

"You're bleeding," she said. "Let me take care of that. I'll be right back. Are you okay to take the controls?"

"Aye, aye, Captain."

Below deck Belle found a sheet that she tore into strips and a bucket she filled with water. Before heading back up, she checked Hunt's bindings. They were still good and tight.

"What's happening?" he asked.

"We're heading back to Charleston."

"Where's Manning?"

"He's on deck."

"Is he all right?" Hunt asked.

"He'll live."

Belle hurried back to Christopher and gently removed his shirt. She cleaned his wound and then expertly wrapped a strip of cloth around it. "You look like a proper pirate now," she teased as she helped him get his shirt back on.

"I don't feel like one."

Belle understood and wanted to put his mind at ease. "I've saved many a man. All were pirates and none expressed their gratitude. Being saved by a woman wasn't something they wished to admit."

"I'd be happy to tell anyone who listened. I was saved by the notorious pirate queen Silver Belle and I will happily show my gratitude. You can have anything you want."

Belle smiled. She knew *exactly* what she wanted.

* * *

CHRISTOPHER'S HEAD was throbbing from where it had hit the deck. He couldn't wait to get back to port. The sky was fully dark and he didn't feel comfortable out here on the open water at night, although he was sure Belle did. Just when he wondered how long it would be until they reached the harbor, the lights of Charleston came into view and as they got closer, he realized they were arriving in time for the Christmas parade of boats.

"Look," Belle said.

"It's the Christmas parade," Christopher said. "We'll have to wait until it's over before we head in. We wouldn't want to interrupt it."

"I want to see it. Those two are fine." Belle stood close to him, weaving her arm through his and resting her head on his shoulder.

"They aren't going to like what awaits them when we get back, so a little more time won't hurt." Christopher leaned his head on hers, happy they were safe and would soon be back among friends.

"The lights are so beautiful," Belle said. "Oh, look at that one!" She pointed out a large yacht strung with colorful lights. The occupants were on deck dressed as Santa and his elves, and enthusiastically waving to everyone. "And that one." The next boat had a large Merry Christmas sign in flashing red lights and trees covered with fake snow. Plastic reindeer in various poses from eating to resting, completed the scene.

Seeing the parade through her eyes made it more special than it had ever been. Christopher had seen the parade many times and it had become old hat, leaving him with little to no enthusiasm for it. In fact, he hadn't even been to the marina to watch it in a few years. Seeing the wonder on Belle's face gave him a whole new appreciation for something that had lost a bit of its luster for him over the years.

When the last boat had approached, Belle reached for his hand and let out a gasp. "It's *The Dagger!*"

"So it is," Christopher said. They waved their arms and Christopher honked the boat's horn to get Edward's attention.

Susanna saw them and poked Edward who turned to see them. Both waved. Edward cupped his hands and yelled. "Where have you been?"

"It's a long story," Christopher shouted back.

The Dagger continued on its course to the dock and Belle guided the boat into a spot next to it and after making sure everything was secure, turned to Christopher.

"We made it," he said. He was wearing an ear-to-ear grin.

Belle wrapped her arms around his neck. "We did." Their lips met as Christopher's hands went to her hips, pulling her close, needing to feel her body nestled against his.

The sound of Manning groaning and Hunt calling from below deck ruined their moment of intimacy.

"Christopher! Belle!" Edward hurried towards them followed by Susanna.

"What happened to you?" Susanna said, pointing to Christopher's shoulder. "We've been so worried."

"We were kidnapped. Manning shot at me, grazing my shoulder. Only a flesh wound. Belle says I'm a proper pirate now." Christopher laughed despite his pain.

"You're lucky his aim was off," Edward said.

"I guess shooting on a boat is different from dry land where nothing's moving," He touched his hand to his now throbbing head, smiling to let them know he was alright and amazed that it seemed to hurt more than his bleeding shoulder.

"You should go get yourself checked out at the E.R." Susanna said.

"What have we here?" Edward pointed to Manning who was squirming around on the deck.

"They followed us to the treasure and were planning to keep it and get rid of us by throwing us overboard."

"Belle stopped them," Christopher said.

"I don't doubt that she did," Edward replied. "One thing I would never do is try to take treasure away from Belle."

"I'm taking Christopher to the hospital," Susanna said.

"Belle and I will see that these two are taken care of," Edward said as he pulled out his phone.

CHAPTER 16

It wasn't a tough sell to convince the police that Manning and Hunt had kidnapped them and tried to take the treasure they'd found. Manning had been secretly under investigation for some time. On every case he was involved in, something would end up missing and eventually the police department put two and two together.

Once his shoulder had been taken care of, both Manning and Hunt were locked away to await trial for this and the many other misdeeds they'd been involved in.

"I'm fine, really, Belle. There's no need to fuss over me," Christopher said.

Belle had spent every waking moment by his side. Her concern for his injury was touching. He loved that she wanted to nurse him back to health, but after being stitched up and told he also had a slight concussion, he could think of so many other ways he would have liked to spend their time together. He never imagined that the Belle he'd met that first day when she'd cursed at him and given him murderous looks would turn into the Belle he was seeing now. Sweet, thoughtful, and gentle were not the words he would have used to describe her then, but they were exactly the words he used now.

She was his angel, much like the one she'd chosen for the top of his tree.

"Tomorrow is Christmas Eve. I've got some shopping to do. I need a few last-minute gifts that I haven't had time to purchase."

"I'll go with you," Belle offered.

"Edward offered to take me." Christopher knew how odd that sounded, but it was the truth. They both had shopping to do for the women in their lives and that meant venturing off on their own to search for the perfect gift. "Besides, Susanna might need your help with the Christmas party."

Belle didn't seem very happy about this pronouncement. "I'd rather go with you and Edward."

"Belle," he hesitated, "you can't. We have some secret business to take care of."

Her eyes narrowed as she cast a sideways glance in his direction. "What are you up to?"

"It's not me," he assured her. "It's Edward. He's looking for something special for Susanna."

"And I cannot go with you?"

"I'm afraid not."

"Belle!" Susanna called down from the main deck. "Would you mind helping me with some party stuff?"

Belle made some unhappy grumblings before answering. "Of course." She leaned down and kissed Christopher as though she might never see him again. Not that he minded. "I don't know what you're up to, but I'll find out."

"I've no doubt you will," he teased.

When she was finally out of sight, he pondered the many ideas he had for her gift. She had all the treasure in the world, but there had to be something he could get that would show her how much she meant to him.

"Are you ready?" Edward appeared at the top of the stairs.

"Ready." Christopher rose and fought off a moment of dizziness.

"You're sure you want to do this?" Edward asked with some concern.

"I'm fine. I just stood up a little too fast."

"While we're out if you don't feel well, just let me know and we'll come back here."

"You pirates are quite the nursemaids." Christopher chuckled.

Edward seemed hurt by this. "Is it wrong for me to be concerned for my good friend?"

"No. Not at all." Christopher gave Edward's shoulder a squeeze.

"Where to first?" Edward asked.

"That depends on what you're looking for."

"I have no idea at all."

Christopher rolled his eyes. "It's going to be a long day."

They started off in the shops near the museum and had gone through almost all of them with no luck.

"I think Susanna would like a piece of jewelry," Edward said.

"I know a little antique store we could try," Christopher suggested.

They took Christopher's car and drove to the outskirts of Charleston, stopping in a shop that looked as antique as anything that might be sold inside.

Edward looked at the jewelry while Christopher looked over a stack of old books in the back of the shop. He leafed through the top few, when his eye caught sight of one called *Female Pirates of the Golden Age.* Gently opening the leather cover, Christopher scanned the contents. About halfway down the page, he saw something he knew would make Belle very happy. Her name was right there in the midst of other famous female pirates of her day. In fact, a full chapter had been dedicated to her story. He wasn't sure he believed in kismet, but it seemed today was his lucky day. He continued looking through the book stacks and came across another book that appealed to him. This one was a journal, handwritten by the author who, like Christopher, had a keen interest in pirates. He dusted off the cover, read the first two pages and decided he would enjoy it more once his head stopped aching. There were a few more books in the stacks that he hadn't checked yet but when he did, he found they were of no interest. Heading to the front of the shop, Christopher was pleased with his finds and hoped Edward had been as lucky.

Edward waved him over as he got closer. He was paying the woman behind the counter for an intensely blue sapphire necklace. The stone was surrounded with a filigree pattern of vines dotted with pearls and diamonds.

"That's beautiful," Christopher said. "Susanna will love it."

"Do you think so?" Edward asked, sounding unsure.

"I think she will. It looks like her."

"What have you got there?"

"A book on female pirates that I think Belle will find fascinating."

"If she's not in it, she won't be happy."

"Oh, she's in it alright. No worries there." Christopher tucked the books under his arm while he waited for the woman to finish wrapping Edward's purchase.

When she was done she did the same for Christopher, wishing them both a very Merry Christmas as they walked out the door.

"What now?" Edward asked.

"There is one more thing I wish I could do for Belle."

"What's that?"

"She left a cat behind on *The Enchantress*. I wish there was a way I could get it for her, but of course that's impossible. I thought I might get one from the local animal shelter. I think having a cat here would make it feel more like home."

"And then you think she might stay," Edward said. He glanced upwards as though thinking. "You know, there might just be a way to get the cat you want, but we'll have to call on Morwenna if she's around and get her involved."

"Do you think she'd be able to retrieve Belle's cat?" Christopher knew all about Morwenna and though he'd never met her, understood that she was the reason both Edward and Belle were now in his life. He was excited to possibly meet her. He'd never known a real witch and the thought of it piqued his curiosity.

"It might take some doing, but if anyone can do it, it would be her."

"It's so close to Christmas. Maybe I should just get her another cat." It wasn't his first choice, but he had a soft spot for the animals at the shelter and if he could liberate one of them for Belle, he'd gladly do so. In fact, he decided that whether they were able to retrieve Belle's cat or not he would adopt one after the holidays. It could be his museum cat. The more he thought about it, the more he liked that idea.

"She had a special connection with One-Eyed Joe, if that's the cat you're talking about." Edward got the car keys out of his pocket.

"You know about him?"

"Of course, everyone did. Let's go see if she's home."

They drove to a secluded area of beach where Morwenna's small one-room cottage stood. There didn't appear to be anyone around. "Do you think there's anyone here?" Christopher asked.

"There's only one way to find out," Edward said. He knocked loudly on the door. "Morwenna! Are you home?" he shouted.

The door flew open and a woman angrily glared at Edward. "What do you want? You're loud enough to wake the dead."

"Oh good," Edward said, ignoring her irritation. "You're here."

Christopher tried not to laugh as Morwenna gave Edward a look that questioned his sanity before looking down the length of her own body and then back at him.

"Do you not see me?" she asked. "Of course I'm here. What do you want?"

Christopher thought it best if he stepped in here before Edward said something that would anger Morwenna even more.

"Morwenna, I'm Christopher Plumb. Not the pirate." He thought he should make that perfectly clear right from the start.

"I can see that," she said, her voice still angry as she glared at Edward, who seemed happily unaware of her irritation and then back to Christopher. "I knew Plumb the pirate. You do look like him though."

"So I've been told. I need your help. You see, Belle Silver left her cat, One-Eyed Joe, on her ship. She really misses him and I was wondering if you could possibly retrieve him for her. I'd like to give him to her as a Christmas gift."

Morwenna's voice and face softened. "You are very sweet to think of her." She gently touched his cheek with her hand. "I'm not sure I can do it. I'd need to go back in time and then find her ship. If it's in port in Bermuda it'll be easy. If it's not there, I'm afraid I wouldn't be able to help you."

Christopher was thrilled Morwenna would even think of doing this for him. The fact that she would travel through time, search the port and deal with the pirates aboard *The Enchantress,* all so he could give Belle a gift spoke volumes about the kind of woman she was. "I understand. Whatever you could do to help would mean the world to me and I know she'd be grateful."

"Tomorrow's Christmas Eve. I'd best head back now. If I find the cat, I'll bring it to *The Dagger.*" She began closing the door.

"Thank you so much," Christopher said.

"Perhaps I can get an invitation to Christmas dinner. What do ye think?" She peered at them through the narrow crack of the door.

Christopher looked to Edward for an answer.

"By all means," Edward said. "We'd be happy to have you join us. In fact, you should come for breakfast too."

"I must be on my way then." She shut the door in their faces. Her voice came from inside. "You might wish to move away from the cottage I don't wish to take you with me."

They did as she suggested, standing far enough away to see what would happen. Nothing did.

"Did it work?" Christopher asked.

"I don't know," Edward said.

"Should we check?"

"Definitely not. If she hasn't gone yet we might get swept up with her."

They decided to be on their way since neither of them was interested in traveling back in time.

* * *

"WHAT ARE you going to do with the treasure now that you've found it?" Susanna asked. She was busy unpacking the groceries they'd picked up after their visit to the caterer.

"I'm not sure. I'll have to think about it." If she stayed here, she wanted Christopher to have it for his museum, or at least most of it. She might consider selling some things so she'd have enough money to live on. But she hadn't decided to stay yet. Did she even want to go back? She'd been so busy with finding the treasure that she really hadn't given it much thought. The way she felt about Christopher had her very much leaning towards staying. She had time to think about it though. It had only been a very short time and if she went back, she would have to be sure it was safe.

"I'm so excited to have you here for Christmas, Belle. We're going to have so much fun." Susanna's joy was contagious.

"Don't you do this every year?" Belle asked.

"Of course, but it's different having guests to share it with." She unloaded the last few things from their shopping trip. "All of this can go in the refrigerator. I hope there's room."

They packed and unpacked the refrigerator until they managed to get everything inside.

"Now, is there anything you'd like to do while we wait for the men to return from getting our presents?"

"Christopher told me Edward was the one who needed to get a gift for you."

"I'm pretty sure Christopher wanted to get something for you too."

"Really? I have nothing for him." A rapid fluttering of butterfly wings erupted in her belly. Belle was delighted that Christopher thought her important enough to go in search of a present for her.

"We can take care of that right now if you like."

"I don't know what I would get him and all I have for money are my silver coins."

"I'll lend you some cash and you can pay me back later when you've sold some of your treasure."

Belle hesitated for a moment. She never liked to be in someone's debt, but with Susanna she felt there was no reason to worry. "If you wouldn't mind."

"I don't mind at all. Let's go then."

They headed off towards the shops Belle had become accustomed to seeing since she'd arrived. There were so many that it was a bit overwhelming. Having no idea what to buy and having so many options made her very unsure.

"Think of it like a treasure hunt," Susanna said.

Belle stopped in her tracks. "I don't need to go shopping, there is something in my father's treasure that I know Christopher would love. I didn't see one in the museum, so perhaps he has never found one."

"Found what?" Susanna asked.

"My father had a pocket watch given to him by a Dutch merchant."

"When you say given, you mean he stole it, right?"

"No. My father took many things over the years, but this watch was a gift he received for rescuing the merchant's daughter from the crew of another pirate ship. The man was so happy to have his daughter back unharmed that he presented my father with his most prized possession."

"What an amazing story and the watch would be an amazing gift. I know Christopher would treasure it and he'll love the story behind it."

"I will need to polish it and find a box to place it in."

"I've got a polishing cloth on the ship, let's find a nice box to put it in."

They headed off to a small gift shop that Susanna assured Belle would have the exact box for the watch.

Belle was thrilled to find so many boxes to choose from. There was one with an inlaid pirate ship on the top. The cover slid off to the side, which made it look as though it didn't open. Only the person who owned the box would know how to remove the lid. "This one is perfect," Belle said to the shop owner.

Susanna paid for it and Belle promised she would pay her back as soon as possible.

Giving and receiving gifts was something she hadn't done in many years and she couldn't believe how excited she was to see the look on Christopher's face when he opened his gift.

Back aboard *The Dagger,* Belle retrieved the watch and polished it up. After so many years underground, she was worried it wouldn't come clean but soon it was shining like new. She placed it in a velvet pouch and nestled it in the puzzle box, then Susanna helped her wrap the gift.

"I can tell you Christopher is going to be the happiest man alive when he sees that watch."

"Do you really think so?" Belle thought so, too, but it was always nice to have someone else confirm it.

"Absolutely. Now we just have to wait for Christmas morning."

CHAPTER 17

The Christmas party aboard *The Dagger* was a hit. Many people from the local business community were there along with friends, Susanna's family and some lucky tourists who happened to be visiting Charleston for the holidays.

"You've outdone yourself yet again," Christopher said, clinking his glass of champagne with Susanna's.

"Why thank you, sir," Susanna said with a curtsy. "I take it you're having fun."

"I think this might just be the best Christmas I've ever had." He'd met Belle, helped find her father's treasure chest, avoided being killed by two low-life detectives and now he was enjoying the merriment of the season with his best friends.

"Wow! That's saying a lot, unless all the others were just miserable affairs." Susanna laughed and waved her hand in front of her face as though she might faint.

"No they were great, but this Christmas I have so much more to celebrate." A serene smile appeared on his lips.

"Are you talking about Belle?" Susanna asked with a hint of teasing.

"How'd you guess? I know we haven't known each other very long, but I believe I've fallen head over heels in love with her."

Susanna tipped her head to the side. "Go on."

"She's unlike anyone I've ever known. She is funny, determined, fiercely loyal and a very good listener. She likes so many of the same things I like. I also think she is the most beautiful woman I've ever known."

"Say no more. I can hear it in your voice and Belle is headed this way."

Christopher's eyes widened at the sight of her. She was glowing in the beautiful silver gown Susanna had given her. Her hair shone in the lights strung across the deck and her eyes, an always changing shade of blue, looked like sapphires tonight. She'd repurposed the silver coins from her clothing into bracelets and earrings and so she jingled, just as she had the first time they'd met.

"Are you enjoying yourself?" Susanna asked as Belle approached them.

"Very much. I was just speaking with your mother and father, Maureen and John. They are lovely people and they are quite taken with Edward."

"They really do love him," Susanna said.

Following her gaze, Christopher could see it had settled on Edward who had just joined her parents.

"If you'll excuse me, I think I'll join them."

Belle moved closer to Christopher. "Do you know, I believe you are the most handsome man at this party."

"Flattery will get you everywhere." He held out his arms to her and she went to him, wrapping her arms around his waist. He kissed the top of her head and held her close. "I'm so happy you're here."

"As am I," Belle replied, gazing up at him.

The blue of her eyes drew him in and held him captive. "I think I'm falling in love with you."

Belle pulled back enough so he could see her face. "No one has ever loved me before."

"How can that be true?"

"Aside from my father, I don't believe I ever allowed anyone the chance, but you are different. It makes me happy to hear you say those words."

Not wanting her to feel pressured to say the same to him, he turned her in his arms so that her back rested on his chest. "Do you know what I like to do at parties like these?" he asked.

Belle shrugged her shoulders. "I don't."

"I like to people watch," he said. "I'm not much of a party person. I prefer a quiet night at home in front of the fireplace with a good glass of brandy."

"Sounds heavenly."

"It is, but I also feel the need to support my friends and so when I am at a party like this one, I usually find a nice quiet spot where I can observe others."

"Is that what we are doing now?" Tipping her head back, she rested it on his shoulder.

Christopher chuckled. "I think it is."

"Good because it is what I like to do as well."

"You're not just saying that, are you?"

"I have not been to many parties. I like being here with you in your embrace and if you wish to stand here like this all night, then I am happy to do the same."

"Then we'll be like two flies on a wall," Christopher said.

"What? I do not wish to be a fly," Belle protested.

"It's just a saying. No one will notice us as we fade into the background."

"If that's what you're hoping, it doesn't seem to have worked."

A man Christopher was unfamiliar with was headed their way.

"Who is that?" he asked.

"I thought it was someone you knew," Belle replied.

The man approached Christopher and handed him a note before turning silently and walking away.

"What was that all about?" Belle asked.

"I'm not sure," Christopher said. He unfolded the paper and much to his surprise it was from Morwenna. She'd found the cat and was waiting for him at her cottage.

"Well?" Belle said.

"It's a note from an old friend who's in town. He's hoping I could meet with him tonight."

"Will you?" she asked.

"Yes. I wish I could take you with me, but I'm afraid he would bore you."

"Alright." Belle moved out of his arms.

"I'll see you tomorrow morning." He pulled her close once again and kissed her. One kiss was definitely not enough and two wouldn't be either, but he had to get to Morwenna's to retrieve One-Eyed Joe so he could present him to Belle the next day at his townhouse. He'd thought about having Morwenna bring the cat when she came for Christmas dinner, but he didn't want Joe to be overwhelmed and thought it would be best to leave him at home.

The look of disappointment on Belle's face hit him in the gut, but it would be worth it when he could give her cat back to her. He lifted her chin with his fingers. "Tomorrow morning."

A soft, sad smile curled Belle's lips. "Tomorrow morning."

Walking away from her in that moment was the hardest thing he'd had to do, but it wasn't for more than the next several hours. He would see her the next day and they would celebrate Christmas together.

* * *

BELLE THOUGHT the whole thing odd, but she checked herself. There was no reason to think Christopher was up to no good. He'd always been truthful with her and the way he'd left her just now with the kiss and the looks, she would be thinking about it until she saw him again.

She headed over to Susanna and Edward with every intention of saying good night.

"Belle, where did Christopher go?" Susanna asked.

"He had to leave. A friend was waiting for him."

"And you let him go?" Edward asked, seeming surprised.

"Of course. I have no reason to doubt him."

"Good, because there is no one more trustworthy than our Christopher," Edward said.

She had to keep reminding herself that unlike the men in her past, Christopher would never do anything to hurt or disappoint her.

"We should say goodbye to our guests. People are starting to leave," Susanna said.

"I'll say good night then," Belle said.

"I know you'll be up bright and early tomorrow morning," Susanna said.

"I'm making French toast for breakfast. You're going to love it," Edward said.

She had no idea what French toast was, but if it was anything like the French fries she'd been introduced to, breakfast would be well worth waking up for. She watched Susanna and Edward walk toward the gangplank, kissing the cheeks and shaking the hands of their departing guests along the way.

As she began to walk to her room, Susanna's parents approached. "I'm so sorry we didn't have more time to chat," Maureen, said as she took Belle's hand. "We'll see you tomorrow though."

"Good night," Belle said.

John, patted her on the shoulder as he passed and within a very short time, the ship was quiet. Belle made her way to her cabin, undressed, and crawled into bed. She couldn't wait to give Christopher his gift in the morning.

* * *

CHRISTOPHER PULLED his car up in front of Morwenna's cottage. He'd gone home first to collect the cat carrier he'd purchased along with a soft, furry blanket for One-Eyed Joe to cuddle with on the trip back to his house. The door to the cottage was open and Morwenna was standing outside waiting for him.

"I'm glad you've arrived. I lost the cat." She stood with her hands on her hips appearing quite perplexed.

"What? How did that happen?" Christopher couldn't believe his ears.

"He's a wily one, he is. I thought I heard you outside and when I opened the door he made a run for it."

Christopher could see that Morwenna was upset about losing the cat and he didn't want to make her feel worse about it. "He couldn't have gone far. Did you see which direction he went in?"

"That way." She pointed toward the beach.

"He shouldn't be too hard to find then. It's all open space."

Christopher trudged through the sand onto the beach. It was completely empty. He turned back to see Morwenna shrugging her shoulders. He looked at the wide-open expanse of beach and thought if he was a cat where would he hide. The fact that it was a dark night with little moonlight wasn't helping. He walked back towards the cottage and heard what he thought might be a cat's soft meow.

"Did you hear that?" he asked.

"I heard nothing," Morwenna said.

"I heard a cat." Christopher moved alongside the walls of the cottage. At the back there was just enough brush to hide a cat, but little chance he could reach in to retrieve it if that's where he was hiding. "One-Eyed Joe are you in there?"

The sound of a soft meow somewhere deep inside the brush reached his ears.

"Stay there," he said. "I've found him, Morwenna. He's in the bushes back here." Christopher came around to the front of the cottage again. "I've got a cat carrier and a can of cat food that should entice him."

Christopher retrieved everything from the car and placed it in front of the bushes. He placed the open can of cat food inside the carrier, hoping the fishy scent would attract Joe. "Come on out, Joe. Belle's waiting for you."

A small pink nose wriggled to and fro as One-Eyed Joe sniffed the cat food from the safety of his hiding spot.

"He's not coming out," Morwenna said.

"Let's give him some time. He doesn't trust us."

"Just like the pirate he is." Morwenna paced back and forth behind Christopher, every now and then releasing a loud sigh of discontent.

"Morwenna, you can go back inside. I'll wait for him to come out." He was afraid with all her moving around and sighing, the cat would stay hidden. "Let's leave him alone for a minute."

He walked just far enough away that he could still see the cat carrier. "Was it hard to find him?"

"Not at all. The ship was still in port. Most of the crew were ashore visiting the local taverns. Those left behind were happy to help me retrieve him. They know how much he means to Belle and they said as much to me."

"I'm glad it wasn't too much trouble for you."

"'Tis Christmas." She shrugged as though running errands through time were just a part of life. "The men of her crew let me know how much they respect her and wish her well. That's saying a lot for a pirate crew. They gave me this note for her." She handed it to Christopher.

"I imagine it is. I'll give this to her when I give her the cat tomorrow evening." He placed the note in his pocket.

"I thought I'd give it to her." Morwenna sounded a bit perturbed.

"How will we explain why you were with her crew?" Christopher asked.

Her face relaxed and she nodded in understanding. "I see what you mean. You will let her know that I helped, won't you?"

"She will definitely know the lengths you went to in retrieving Joe."

Morwenna seemed quite pleased with his response. "Thank you."

The bushes rattled. Slowly and with great caution, the cat emerged. He was a gray tabby, as Belle had described him, with one turquoise colored eye and one eye that appeared to be closed.

"Well, hello there," Christopher said. He held his hand out to the cat who pulled back slightly before taking the opportunity to sniff his hand. After a few tentative moments he allowed Christopher to softly pet his head before emerging completely from the brush.

"Are you hungry? I brought you some food." Christopher gestured to the can inside of the carrier and waited for Joe to enter. Once he did, he closed the door feeling a sense of accomplishment. "I'll take him home, let him get settled. I can't wait to see Belle's face when she sees him." He took one last look at the cat and then turned to Morwenna. "Would you like a ride to breakfast?"

"I would like that."

Christopher stood and lifted the carrier. "I'll see you in the morning then." He turned to her one last time before he left. "You did a good thing sending Belle to this time."

"Because she found her treasure?" Morwenna tipped her head as she looked at him.

"Not just that. All the jewels and coins were more than she could have hoped for, but the best thing was the connection it gave her to her father. The letter in the chest meant more to her than anything else of value within."

"And what about you?" she asked.

"I don't know what you mean?" Christopher was puzzled by her question. He hadn't traveled through time and finding the treasure had been amazing, but it was Belle's treasure. Then a lightbulb went off. He understood what she was asking. "Belle is the best thing to happen to me in ages. She is an amazing woman. I think I fell in love with her the very first moment I saw her, even though she had just broken into my museum." He chuckled at the memory.

"Belle is lucky to have found you." Morwenna said, placing her hand on his arm.

"I think it's the other way around. I'm the lucky one."

"I like you more and more each time I meet you," she let go of his arm and smiled warmly at him.

"I feel the same about you." He surprised her with a quick peck on the cheek before heading to his car.

Placing the cat carrier in the front seat in a way that allowed Joe to see him, he got in the driver's seat. Morwenna waved to him as he backed his car up and turned around heading for home.

"Well, Joe, it's just the two of us tonight. Belle is going to be so happy to see you in the morning."

Back at his townhouse, Christopher let Joe out of the carrier to explore. He had been sure to pick up everything he would need to care for the cat. Joe sniffed around the house and batted at the ornaments on the low branches of the Christmas tree.

Christopher retrieved the journal he found at the antique shop and made himself comfortable on the sofa. The author was someone who, like himself, had a great interest in the Golden Age of Piracy, especially hidden treasure. The clerk at the antique shop had mentioned that it was brought in by a woman clearing out her deceased grandfather's attic. From the looks of it, it was written sometime in the early twentieth century. As he read the first few pages, Joe jumped on the sofa and curled up beside him before falling asleep. Christopher ran his hand along Joe's soft fur, careful not to disturb him.

Leafing through the pages, Christopher found a pocket towards the back with several pieces of paper that had been neatly folded. Unfolding them he found not one or two, but several hand drawn maps that appeared to be treasure maps. There were no notations as to where they came from or who they belonged to, but their mere presence thrilled Christopher. He couldn't wait to share them with Belle. Neatly folding them, he placed them back where he found them and then put the journal in his coat pocket so he wouldn't forget it in the morning. It was an exciting find and one that could mean months, if not years of treasure hunting in his future or, as he hoped, their future.

CHAPTER 18

The smell of something delicious pulled Belle from her bed earlier than she had expected. Quickly washing up and putting on an outfit Susanna had given her for this special day, Belle looked herself over in the mirror. The blue velvet of the dress highlighted her eyes. Her hair was brushed to a glossy, but slightly tousled state, one she thought would entice Christopher. One last look in the mirror and the scent from the galley was calling to her. Coffee, bacon and sugary sweetness tickled her nose as she quickened her pace.

"Good morning," Susanna said. She was stationed at the stove, which was not the norm aboard *The Dagger*.

"Good morn. Where's Edward?" Belle asked, glancing around and not seeing him.

"He'll be right back. Don't worry. I'm just minding the stove for him so that nothing burns." Susanna's warm smile let her know that she had taken no offense to Belle's obvious concern. "He had to get some champagne from below deck."

The galley, which was also the main living space had been decorated with lights and Christmas baubles. The Christmas tree was settled into a corner and piled high with boxes wrapped in red and green paper.

"So many presents," Belle said.

"Gifts for everyone, my parents and our crew included. The crew will get theirs tomorrow."

"You and Edward are quite generous."

"We want them to know we appreciate them and that they're part of our family."

She thought about her crew. They had their own wives and children, but when they were aboard *The Enchantress* they were a big family, who behaved in all the ways that close relatives did. They laughed with each other, celebrated, and also fought—but never for very long. She missed them. This was the first time she'd really thought about them since she'd left. She was unsure of when she could return or if she even would, but she hoped they had a Merry Christmas and were exactly where they wanted to be.

Edward returned, champagne bottles in hand. "Your parents are here. I saw them walking towards the ship."

"If you open those, I'll get those mimosas started so we can hand them one when they walk in."

Edward opened the bottles while Susanna retrieved the glasses.

"How are you this morning, Belle?" Edward asked.

"Well, thank you." She wouldn't allow her moments of reminiscing ruin what promised to be a joyful occasion.

A moment later and the sounds of people excited to be together filled the air. Belle greeted Susanna's parents and as they made their way into the galley, she was overjoyed and surprised to see Christopher arriving with Morwenna. She couldn't take her eyes off him and it seemed he was doing the same.

* * *

CHRISTOPHER SPOTTED BELLE RIGHT AWAY. She looked stunning in a beautiful blue dress. Her feet were bare. She hadn't taken to wearing the heels Susanna had gotten her and instead chose to go without shoes while aboard the ship. He scooped her up into his arms, being careful not to step on her toes.

"Good morning," he whispered into her ear, before kissing her cheek.

She leaned her cheek into his. "Good morning."

"Merry Christmas!" he said to those in the room.

A chorus of Merry Christmas came from everyone back to him.

"Morwenna, I'm surprised to see you," Belle said.

"I'm surprised to be here. It was good of Edward to invite me."

Christopher took his coat off and hung it on a hook by the door. He'd left the cat at home where he seemed happy. His hope was to surprise Belle later that day by bringing her home with him for a quiet Christmas night by the fire.

"Everything smells delicious," Christopher said as Edward handed him a mimosa. "Thank you."

"Merry Christmas to us all," Edward raised his glass and everyone joined him.

Christopher was thrilled that Belle had wrapped an arm around his waist and seemed quite comfortable there.

"Shall we have some breakfast and then open our presents?" Susanna said.

Everyone took their places at the table. Excellent food and conversation filled their bellies and their hearts. When the last piece of French toast had been split between Christopher and Edward and the plate that had held the bacon was empty, they all moved to sit around the Christmas tree. The scent of pine filled the room.

"I love the smell of a fresh tree," Christopher said.

"It does smell nice," Belle replied.

"I'll go first," Edward said. He handed Susanna his neatly wrapped package.

"I wonder what it is?" she asked.

"Open it," her mother encouraged.

Her mouth fell open as she lifted the beautiful sapphire necklace from the box.

Christopher winked at Edward who seemed quite pleased with himself.

"It's beautiful! I love it!" Susanna gushed. "Now it's my turn." She handed Edward his gift.

Opening it, he was delighted to find the hammock he'd been wanting.

"So you can nap on deck whenever you want. It's handmade here in Charleston and the quilted fabric is a special kind that can withstand the sun and weather."

"Thank you, love. It's perfect."

Christopher went next, giving Belle her gift.

She gave him a questioning glance. "Go on. Open it."

"Belle removed the book from the wrappings and read the title. She looked at Christopher with a smile that seemed to say she wasn't sure why he'd chosen it for her.

"If you open to page fifty-two you'll see the reason for this gift." He moved closer so that their shoulders touched and watched her face as she opened the book.

Belle turned to the page Christopher had suggested and read aloud her name at the top of the page. Her smile widened into a huge grin. "It's me," she whispered. "They've written about me."

"It's a pretty lengthy chapter. I think you'll be pleased with what the author has to say."

"I'll read it later," she said. Leaning in she kissed his cheek. "Thank you. This is such a special gift and you were so thoughtful to find it for me."

He whispered in her ear, "I've got something else for you at my townhouse. I thought we could go there later."

"I'd like that," Belle replied. "I've got something for you." She handed him the gift wrapped box, which he opened. "It's a puzzle box," she explained.

"I love it," he replied. He loved puzzles. In fact, he'd always thought of archeology as a sort of puzzle – searching for clues and putting the pieces together to come up with a story.

"See if you can open it." The excited look on her face had Christopher wondering if something might be inside.

After a few moments of tinkering with it, the box opened and much to his surprise he found a velvet bag inside. Lifting it out, he felt the weight of it in his hands and upon opening the bag he found a silver pocket watch. The face was painted with a scene of ship on the ocean with a starry night sky. "Oh, Belle, this is too generous of you."

"I want you to have it. It belonged to my father and I'm sure he would be pleased to know that it now belongs to you."

He could hardly speak. Christopher's heart was overflowing with so many feelings. This was quite a special gift she had given him. It said something about how she viewed him. To give him something that was special to her father said so much about how she felt.

"Do you like it?" Belle asked, seeming unsure.

"I love it and I love that you entrusted me with your father's pock-etwatch."

"Tell him how your father got it," Susanna suggested.

"He rescued a Dutch merchant's daughter from another pirate crew and her father gave it to him in thanks for saving his daughter's life."

"That makes it all the more special," Christopher said.

The others continued with the gift exchange. There was even something for Morwenna. Edward and Susanna got her the largest box of chocolates they could find. Morwenna literally jumped for joy upon receiving it.

As for Christopher, all he wanted was Belle by his side. "Belle, I found something else yesterday that I thought might interest you."

"What would that be?" she asked.

He hopped up and retrieved his jacket where he pulled the journal from its pocket.

"What's that you've got there?" Edward asked.

"It's the journal I picked up yesterday at the antique book shop." He opened it to the pouch where he'd placed the maps and removed them. "Look what I found inside."

Everyone gathered around as he opened one and held it out for them to see.

Edward took it and examined it. "It's a treasure map!"

"They all are," Christopher said as he continued unfolding the maps. He handed one to Belle and laid the others out in front of him. "What do you think? Would you go treasure hunting with me again?"

"I would love that," Belle said.

"Can I join you?" Edward asked.

"Of course," Christopher said after checking with Belle who nodded her agreement.

"If Edward's going, then I am too," Susanna said.

"We wouldn't think of going without you," Christopher said. He turned to Belle. "This could take some time. Do you think you'll be staying around to go on all these hunts with me?" He hoped with all his heart she'd say yes.

"I can't think of anything I'd rather do." Belle moved closer to Christopher and laid her head on his shoulder.

"It's settled then. The four of us will be starting our very own treasure hunting venture."

"That's quite exciting," Susanna's father said.

"If we can help in any way, let us know," Maureen added.

"I'd be happy to help as well. You never know what a witch can do for you," Morwenna added.

They examined each of the maps for the next couple of hours, taking a break to enjoy the delicious Christmas turkey that Edward had prepared for them.

"You've outdone yourself, my friend," Christopher said. "I might have to take some lessons from you. That way you don't have to do all the cooking for this group of treasure hunters."

"It would be my pleasure," Edward replied, his excitement obviously bubbling over, "Let's get back to those maps."

They all chatted excitedly, making plans to do research that might shed light on exactly who these maps belonged to and where the treasure might be hidden. They had tentative thoughts about it, but it was agreed that they would talk more after the holidays.

"We should really get going," Christopher said, gazing at Belle. "Morwenna can we drop you off at your cottage?"

"I'll take her back," Edward said. "You go enjoy what's left of the day."

They said their goodbyes and headed off. Christopher could hardly wait to see the look on Belle's face when she saw her present.

* * *

This had been one of the best days of her life so far. Going home with Christopher meant that the day and the night were about to get even better.

Arriving at his home, Christopher unlocked the door and held it open for her to enter.

A quiet meow came from the other room.

"What was that?" Belle asked, thinking for a moment it sounded like One-Eyed Joe.

"It sounds like a cat," Christopher said, holding back a chuckle.

"I didn't know you had a cat," Belle said, gazing at him with narrowed eyes and a furrowed brow.

"I don't."

"What? Then how…"

Just then a gray tabby cat with one eye trotted into the room. Belle's hands flew to her mouth. "Joe? Is that you?"

"Merry Christmas," Christopher said.

Belle dropped to her knees as Joe approached and then hopped right into her arms. She held him close, nuzzling his fur with her nose. Tears trickled down her cheeks. "Oh, Joe. I thought I'd never see you again. Can you forgive me for leaving you behind?"

"From the sounds of that purring, I think he definitely has," Christopher said.

"How? Why?" Belle was so touched by Christopher's gesture.

"It wasn't all me. Morwenna helped. I merely asked if she could possibly get your cat for you. She was happy to do it."

"I wish I had known so that I could have thanked her."

"We can thank her the next time we see her. She also brought this." He extracted a folded paper from his pocket. "For you."

Belle opened it and began reading. It was from her quartermaster, Samuel Stone. "He says my men are all well and happy, though they miss me. The English captain is still searching for me and has sworn to continue until he finds me. He'd been aboard the ship and when he couldn't locate me there, left them with a warning that he'd be back to check again. Samuel feels it would be unsafe for me to come back and wishes me well here in this time." It was clear to Belle that her choice had been a good one and even though she could not return, it really didn't upset her as it would have not so long ago. She folded the note and set it down.

"You have made me so happy in so many ways today," Belle said. "I don't know how to thank you."

He joined Belle on the floor as she held onto Joe. "You make me so happy Belle, having you in my life is all the thanks I need. I've fallen in love with you Belle."

"Oh, Christopher. I love you, too. It didn't take long for me to discover the man you truly are and just how special you are to me. I can't imagine my life without you in it."

"I told you I wasn't the Christopher Plumb you once knew," he teased.

"You are not that man, but he couldn't be all bad because without him, there would be no you and I would be all the poorer because of it." She leaned over and kissed him. Joe, however, had other plans. He managed to weasel his way between them and up to their faces where he kept them from the kissing marathon that was about to happen.

They couldn't help but laugh.

"Let's sit by the fire," Christopher said, as he got the fireplace going.

"I'm amazed by that. With the push of a button a fire is started."

"I can't wait to show you all the other amazing things you never thought possible." He stood up, "I'll be right back. You sit there with Joe and enjoy the fire."

Joe curled himself into a ball and made himself at home on Belle's lap as she stared into the fire thinking how fortunate she was to be here in this time with the man she loved. Leaving the world she knew behind wasn't so hard knowing that her new life was just beginning and it was going to be better than she could have ever hoped.

Christopher returned with two cups of hot chocolate. Christmas music played in the background as he handed her a mug and sat beside her, wrapping his arm around her shoulder. They stayed that way, enjoying the music, the hot chocolate and especially each other's company for a good long time before leaving Joe on his own to do what cats do at night and heading upstairs where Belle would spend the night in the arms of the man she loved.

A NOTE FROM JENNAE

Thank you so much for reading Silver Belle. If you enjoyed this story and have a minute to spare, I would really appreciate a short review on the page or site where you bought the book. Your help in spreading the word is greatly appreciated. Reviews from readers like you make a huge difference in helping new readers find stories similar to Silver Belle.

If you'd like to know when my next book comes out and want to receive occasional updates from me, then you can sign up for my newsletter here: https://www.subscribepage.com/w4j6s3

ACKNOWLEDGMENTS

As always I'd like to thank my editor, Jen Graybeal and my cover artist, Sheri McGathy.

ABOUT THE AUTHOR

Jennae Vale is a best selling author of romance with a touch of magic. As a history buff from an early age, Jennae often found herself daydreaming in history class and wondering what it would be like to live in the places and time periods she was learning about. Writing time travel romance has given her an opportunity to take those daydreams and turn them into stories to share with readers everywhere.

Originally from the Boston area, Jennae now lives in the San Francisco Bay area, where some of her characters also reside. When Jennae isn't writing, she enjoys spending time with her family and her pets, and daydreaming, of course.

www.jennaevaleauthor.com

ALSO BY JENNAE VALE

THE THISTLE & HIVE SERIES

A Bridge Through Time

A Thistle Beyond Time

Saved By Time

A Matter of Time

A Turn In Time

All In Good Time

A Long Forgotten Time

Awakened By Time

Saved By Time

In Time For Edna

A Thistle & Hive Christmas

THE MACKALLS OF DUNNET HEAD

Her Trusted Highlander

Her Noble Highlander

Her Mysterious Highlander

THE DELIGHT SERIES

Ross (Prequel)

Wanted

Watched

Wounded

Christmas In Delight

The Whisperer

THE GREEN SKY SERIES

The Dagger (Prequel)

Green Sky At Night

The Golden Hook

Silver Belle

EDNA'S WORLD

Love Set Apart

OTHER BOOKS

A Highlander In Vegas

9 798369 900024